MR. DARCY IN TIME

A PRIDE AND PREJUDICE TIME TRAVEL VARIATION

ADA BYRN

Cover image by jayjaneanea/depositphotos.com

✾ Created with Vellum

1

———————

THE BEGINNING

FITZWILLIAM DARCY
March 1843

THE GREEKS BELIEVED in the Fates, three old women who spin the threads of human destiny. Clotho spun the thread, Lachesis dispensed it, and Atropos cut it, determining a person's moment of death.

As I celebrate my sixtieth birthday, I have been contemplating my strange and complicated life. I think sometimes that my thread was full of knots, and I hope that it will be much longer before it is cut off.

For the sake of my posterity, I have determined

to write down my amazing experiences so that my children may understand me better, and hopefully learn from my mistakes. My greatest wish is that they may be wiser and happier than their father and grandfather.

Whether they will believe my tale remains to be seen.

If I had not lived it, I would not have believed it myself.

THERE WAS nothing in my birth or early childhood to foreshadow the adventures I would have. I was born in the year of 1783 to goodly parents. My father, Mr. George Darcy, was the landowner of Pemberley, a large estate in Derbyshire, and my mother, Lady Anne, was the second daughter of the Earl of Matlock.

My parents were both excellent people. My mother was beautiful, bright, and creative. She had a warm heart. She loved to laugh. She loved me as a child and for many years, I was an only child and, unlike many women of her generation and particularly women of status, my mother took the time to parent me. I had the usual wet nurse and nannies, but Lady Anne always listened to me. She wanted to know everything I was learning and doing.

My father was, without exception, the most remarkable man I have ever met. He was a learned man. He was always reading. He was interested in science and did everything he could to make Pemberley profitable and efficient. He was an excellent landlord, an excellent master, and an excellent father.

He seemed to have the patience of Job and the wisdom of Solomon. If ever there was a problem, he would look at it calmly and rationally, ask the appropriate questions, and then make decisions that were incredibly insightful.

Once when I was a young lad, I climbed a tree and fell, breaking my arm. I was obviously upset, distraught, but a local doctor set the bone and I remember my father sitting beside my bed, telling me not to worry. He said that God in his wisdom had created our bodies such that they could heal and that although I would have to restrict my activities for a season, afterwards I would be whole again. His calm assurance did much to lessen my fears. He gave me hope. Our conversation that day was one I often recalled when I was discouraged.

As he told me, "Son, life has its trials and its

tribulations. And oft times, the best thing you can do is just to accept it and try to find a way to make things better."

And I said, "How can I make my arm better? How can I make this better?"

He ruffled my hair with his hand. "Well, because you are not going to be running about as much, this could give you more time to practice your Latin or your Greek. But not the pianoforte, I think."

Naturally, I laughed at his joke, which illustrated my father's mature and good-natured approach to life.

The rest of my youth was not remarkable. A few months before my eleventh birthday, my sister Georgiana was born. My mother died a day later, due to complications of the birth.

When my father told me, I cried. My father patted my shoulder and said, "Every day with your mother was a blessing. And now we must go forward."

Later, I attended Cambridge and then in 1806, I received a letter from Mrs. Reynolds, the house-keeper at Pemberley, informing me that my father was ill, most possibly dying and that I must return home.

I shall never forget the day he died. I sat in the master bedroom at Pemberley, sitting next to my father's bed just as he had often sat by mine when I was ill. The bed curtains were open, but the room was dark, lit only by the fireplace and a few candles.

My father lay still with his eyes closed. The physician had already seen to my father and bled him twice, but there was no improvement. He said my father had a growth in his abdomen, a cancer, and that there was nothing further he could do.

"Would surgery help?"

"No. It would kill him."

My father's skin was pale, and his breath was shallow. I feared that every shuddering breath would be his last.

I had so many fears and doubts. I was only twenty-three years of age. I was not ready to be Master of Pemberley, and yet, that fate would soon be thrust upon me.

I could hear Georgiana crying outside in the hallway. She was sitting with her governess. She had already said her farewells. She was so young. What would she do without both her parents? My heart sank with the weight of responsibility that awaited me. I and my cousin Richard would be Georgiana's guardians. I would be both Father and Brother to her now.

There were so many things I wanted to say to my father, to thank him for my life and all that he had done for me, but the words stuck in my throat. I was afraid that if I said the words, they would be final, and then he would slip away from me into the great beyond.

I was not a particularly religious man, for I preferred science, but at that moment, I prayed.

If there was a God and a heaven, my father should go there.

"Fitzwilliam," my father said weakly.

I leaned closer to my father's lips. "Yes, sir?"

"My watch."

My father had always worn a watch on a fob at his waist, but now he was in his nightshift.

I looked about the room and saw the watch on a table beside the bed, where there was a pitcher of water in a basin and cloths.

"Do you wish to know what time it is, sir?" I asked.

"No. Give it … to you."

I walked to the table and handed the ornate watch to my father, who held it briefly in his hands and then passed it to me with trembling fingers.

"It … is … yours … now."

I thanked him, telling him that I would treasure it. As I looked at it more closely, I saw that the time was incorrect. I made a motion to adjust the time, and my father said, "No. Doesn't work that way."

His few words were said in almost a whisper.

I could not help but smile. "What is the good of it then? A watch that does not tell time?"

"It is not an average watch. It can enable you to go back in time."

I frowned, not understanding what I was hearing. What nonsense was this? Was my father making a joke on his deathbed? "I beg your pardon?"

My father sighed. "I know you will not believe. But it is true." As he continued to talk about the watch, he seemed to gain energy.

I decided to humor him. I said gently, "What a fantastical idea, to go back in time."

My father said earnestly, "Yes, but I promise you it is not foolishness. It is real. If you wish to go back in time, you hold the watch in your hand, tight in your fist, close your eyes and imagine the time you wish to go to. It must be a specific memory, with a specific time and a specific place, otherwise, it will not work."

He spoke fervently, but the last sentence seemed

to tax his strength, and he coughed and then groaned with pain.

I held the watch in my hand. I did not want to agitate him. I said, "If you could go back in time, why do you not do so now? You could live longer."

My father closed his eyes. "I already have."

Well, that certainly made a kind of sense. But I thought it more likely that pain and suffering had made my father delirious. I also knew that he had been dosed with laudanum which could cause hallucinations.

"How did you obtain this watch?" I asked.

"It has been in the family for generations, passing from father to eldest son."

"How can that be? Are you telling me that all of my ancestors, everyone in the portrait gallery, has had the ability to go back in time?"

My father gave a short laugh that sounded more like a croak. "Why else do you think we are so wealthy? How else could I have won the hand of your mother? Lady Anne was the daughter of an earl, and I was a lowly farmer."

"Hardly that, sir." The Darcy family holdings were vast, and my father's income was more than ten thousand pounds a year.

My father continued, "My time is running

short, but I have no fear. I have lived a long and useful life, three or four times as long as any man should live, and I have no regrets."

"It is a rare man who can say that."

"I look forward to Paradise with your mother and your younger brother, Michael."

I had a younger brother, who had been born a few years before Georgiana who had only lived a few months.

I clutched my father's hand. "Please, sir. Do not go, yet."

For a few minutes he was quiet, but then he rallied and said clearly, "Be careful, Fitzwilliam. The watch is a blessing, but it can also be a curse, for once you go back, you cannot go forward. You must relive your past and you must be very careful." He looked at me as if he could see into my very soul and see all my faults and weaknesses. "But I am not worried. I believe you will be wise. You have always been a good, dutiful son. I have no doubt that you will take excellent care of Pemberley and your sister."

"Thank you, sir."

My father closed his eyes and did not speak again.

A few hours later, his breath became heavy, and

he slipped into unconsciousness, and then later, death.

I looked at the watch. My father had worn it every day of his life, and I would do the same, to honor his memory.

Did I think that the watch could send me back in time?

Absolutely not.

No one could travel back in time. That was nonsense.

2

MEETING MISS ELIZABETH BENNET

OVER THE NEXT FEW YEARS, I spent the majority of my efforts taking care of my sister Georgiana and managing Pemberley. In October 1811, I went to Hertfordshire to visit my good friend Charles Bingley. He had recently rented Netherfield Park and wished me to see it. I had my reservations, because I did not want to spend too much time with his unmarried sister, Caroline. Miss Bingley, like many of the young women in London society, found me attractive. Not for my appearance, my individual character or my talents, but for my fortune. I knew that if I spent time at Bingley's estate, I ran the risk of Miss Bingley's matchmaking plans.

I planned to spend two months there and return to Darcy House in London before Christmas.

However, while there, I met a young woman who would change the trajectory of my life. Her name was Elizabeth Bennet, and she was then, only twenty years of age.

I saw her first at an Assembly, but at the time I was an arrogant fool. I was not impressed with her at all. I scarcely allowed her to be pretty, and when Bingley suggested that I dance with her, I rudely declined, declaring that she was tolerable, but not handsome enough to tempt me. Miss Elizabeth was sitting out, instead of dancing, and I said that I was in no humor to give consequence to young ladies who were slighted by other men.

I learned later that she had overheard our conversation.

Now, those words bring me nothing but shame, but I confess – such was my pride and conceit at the time, that I did not recognize her true worth.

But over the next few weeks, I saw more of Miss Elizabeth at dinners and parties where Bingley and I were invited.

I saw that she was intelligent, and she had the most beautiful dark eyes. Her figure was light and pleasing, and although her manners were not of the fashionable world, I was caught by their easy playfulness.

I began to watch Miss Elizabeth more closely, listening to her conversations. I wanted to know her better, and yet, I was appalled by her family and her inferior connections.

Miss Elizabeth had two uncles in Trade. One, Mr. Phillips, was an attorney living in Meryton. The other, Mr. Gardiner, owned a large warehouse and sold furnishings from a shop near Cheapside. Mr. Bennet was a gentleman farmer, with a tidy estate called Longbourn. Mr. Bennet was something of a scholar with a clever turn of phrase, but I did not approve of Mrs. Bennet. I thought she was vulgar and loud. She wanted to find husbands for her five daughters, and I saw only her silliness and desperation.

Miss Elizabeth had an older sister, Jane, who was the acknowledged beauty of the family. She was fair-haired and sweet-natured. My friend Bingley was immediately attracted to her.

At the time, Bingley was only twenty-two years of age, and I thought he was too young to consider marriage. Besides that, he was easily distracted. I had seen him fall in love twice before, so I did not expect his infatuation to last.

During a visit to Netherfield Park, Jane caught a cold and had to stay there several days to recover.

Her sister Elizabeth came to see her and stayed as well.

It was during this time, seeing Elizabeth daily at breakfast and dinner, that I fell in love with her. I admired her clever wit and strength of character. She liked to argue with me and had a habit of lifting her chin and glancing at me defiantly as if daring me to respond.

Unlike the many women in London, she did not flatter me.

I was enchanted, besotted, and I knew I must leave before making a shocking misalliance.

So, in late November, after Bingley's ball, I returned to London, determined to put temptation behind me.

Over the next few months, I thought of Elizabeth often, especially after learning from Miss Bingley that Jane Bennet was in Town, living with the Gardiners.

I must have driven past Mr. Gardiner's shop a dozen times, but I could not make myself enter and enquire about his niece.

All I could think of was how my family and friends would respond if I married Elizabeth. They would think I was a fool to marry beneath my station. And frankly, I feared that if I married Elizabeth, she might grow to become like her mother. Over my short life, I had seen too many men marry a sweet girl, only to find that the apple doesn't fall far from the tree.

Daily I considered telling Bingley that he should return to Netherfield Park and take me with him.

How my life would have differed if I had admitted my love then, I do not know.

Then in early April 1812, I travelled with my cousin Richard, Colonel Fitzwilliam, to Rosings Park in Kent to visit my aunt, Lady Catherine de Bourgh, the older sister of my mother.

Lady Catherine was a tall woman who ruled her household and the surrounding neighbors with an iron will. My cousin Richard often joked that she should have been a warrior queen like Boadicea, and I could well imagine her armed with sword and shield as she made her pronouncements.

At the breakfast table one day, she informed us that her parson, Mr. Collins had married a Miss Lucas a few months earlier and that they were currently entertaining guests: Mrs. Collins' father, Sir William Lucas, her younger sister Miss Maria Lucas, and a friend of Mrs. Collins – one Miss Elizabeth Bennet.

The name of my love seemed to pierce my heart like a dagger.

At that moment, Elizabeth was less than a mile away. I had to see her again. With careful composure, I said that I had met Mrs. Collins previously and that I should visit her – as a matter of politeness.

Richard looked at me as if I had gone mad. He knew that I had little patience for most of society's foolish rules.

"You want to call on them?" he said in astonishment.

"I do."

"Then I will go with you," he declared.

Lady Catherine said that she liked Mrs. Collins. "She is plain, but she has sense. I think Mr. Collins chose well when he married her. When he first went to Longbourn, he planned to marry one of the Bennet girls. From the gossip of the parsonage servants, it appears that he proposed first to Miss Elizabeth Bennet, but she refused him."

This news was another blow.

What would I have done if Mr. Collins had married her? If she had belonged to another man?

I could not bear the thought.

At that moment, I knew that I wanted Elizabeth for myself, regardless of the consequences.

My aunt continued, saying, "I don't know why Miss Bennet was so foolish. Mr. Collins would have made her an excellent husband, particularly since he will one day inherit her family home. But, overall, I am glad that she did not accept his offer. She is a pretty girl but pert. She expresses her opinions forthrightly without proper deference to her elders."

I had to hide a smile, knowing that Elizabeth would be amused by Lady Catherine's imperious nature. Elizabeth had a quick humor like her father and often found amusement in absurdities.

As soon as we finished breakfast, Richard and I walked over to the parsonage. "Who is this Miss Elizabeth Bennet?" he teased. "Shall I like her?"

I glared at him. "You had best not."

He whistled. "So, is that the way it is? You have fallen in love with her?"

I would not answer him, and he laughed at me.

When we arrived at the parsonage, I sat like a block, saying little, because I felt tongue tied before her. Elizabeth was even more beautiful than I had remembered. There was so much I wanted to say to her, but what could I say in public other than asking about her family?

Richard was more at ease and chatted comfortably.

I could tell that Elizabeth enjoyed his company and I was unreasonably jealous, which made me even more awkward.

The next few days were both a thrill and a torment. The Collins's and Elizabeth came to Rosings for coffee or dinner several times. I learned that Elizabeth liked to take walks in the grounds around Rosings, so I took walks as well, acting pleasantly surprised to see her, not letting her know that I was walking with the sole purpose of meeting her.

I will never forget those days. I was besotted. I burned for her. I tossed and turned at night, wanting to declare myself.

And yet I held back, inwardly fighting with myself.

Finally, one afternoon, the dam broke. After hearing from Mrs. Collins that Elizabeth was at the parsonage with a headache, I called on her.

I shall never forget how she looked, sitting at a table and rising to her feet as a servant announced me.

The sun streamed through curtains and she looked like a goddess in her long white dress. Her hair was styled up on her head with pink ribbons winding through her dark curls.

I told her boldly that I loved her. "In vain have I struggled. It will not do. My feelings will not be repressed. You must allow me to tell you how ardently I admire and love you."

She was astonished and for a moment, silent.

I told her how I had struggled, knowing the vast differences between her family and my own, acknowledging her inferiority. But all of that was nothing to me because I loved her so passionately. I ended by expressing my hope that my agony would now be rewarded by her acceptance of my hand.

When she spoke, her cheeks were flushed, and her words were measured. "In such cases as this, it is, I believe the established mode is to express a sense of obligation for the sentiments avowed, however unequally they may be returned. I know I should thank you for the compliment, but I cannot. I have never desired your good opinion, and you have certainly bestowed it most unwillingly. I am sorry to give you pain, but I hope it will be of a short duration."

I could not believe what I was hearing. Was Elizabeth refusing me?

I said stiffly, "And this is all the reply which I am

to have the honor of expecting! I might, perhaps, wish to be informed why, with so little endeavor at civility, I am thus rejected. But it is of small importance."

She then turned on me, saying that if she was uncivil, it was nothing compared to my incivility. How could I propose to her after denigrating her family? She also accused me of separating her sister Jane from Bingley — which I had done — and she spoke of my arrogance and how I had treated George Wickham abominably.

The name of my prior friend and current enemy made me livid. I retorted, "You take an eager interest in that gentleman's concerns."

Elizabeth returned hotly, "Who that knows what his misfortunes have been, can help feeling an interest in him?'

At this point, I was so angry, so offended, I could not hold back. I said that perhaps I should have lied to her, hidden my struggles and flattered her, so that she would have accepted my offer. "But disguise of every sort is my abhorrence."

Her face grew pale and when she spoke, it was as if her words were ice. "You are mistaken, Mr. Darcy if you suppose that the mode of your declaration affected me in any other way, than as it spared me the concern which I might have felt in refusing you, had you behaved in a more gentleman-like manner."

Good God.

I hardly know what else I said, but the conversation ended with Elizabeth declaring that I was the last man in the world that she could have ever been prevailed upon to marry.

I left the parsonage, my hat and gloves in my hand. I marched halfway to Rosings, then turned back, then turned back again.

I could not think.

How could this have happened?

I thought Elizabeth had been flirting with me, that she admired me, that she liked me and that she would be pleased to become my wife.

I could not believe what had just happened.

It was all George Wickham's fault. That man. That evil man who had almost eloped with Georgiana and lied every other sentence. He had deceived Elizabeth and poisoned her mind so she believed that I had cruelly denied Wickham his living.

I could not understand how she could believe Wickham, Wickham who was so slick, so smooth. How could anyone believe him? And yet she had.

I was a damn fool.

Why had I said all those things about her family?

I was madly in love, but I had spoken in haste, not thinking it through.

I had been overcome by my feelings, and I had blurted them out, without thought, without purpose.

If only I had been more circumspect.

If only I had spoken calmly, more reasonably.

I could have explained about Wickham and won her over.

But perhaps not. She was angry that I separated Bingley and her sister. Damn Richard for telling Elizabeth about Bingley. He was the only way she could have known it, and Richard had told me earlier that he had walked and talked with her that day.

When I thought about Bingley, I thought angrily that I had been kinder to him than I had been to myself. That I had saved him from being trapped by a Bennet.

I wished I had never gone to Netherfield Park, never met Elizabeth, never fallen in love with her.

The pain I felt was too bitter.

I was furious.

And how could she say such things about me – that I was not behaving like a gentleman?

But the longer I stood there, the more I knew that she was correct. Her words had wounded my pride.

I was a proud man. I often thought poorly of my fellow men and thought I was superior.

But in Elizabeth's eyes, I was inferior.

What could I do?

Out of habit, I glanced at my father's watch hanging on the fob at my waist. I glanced at the hands that never moved. I wished my father were here, so he could give me advice – tell me what to do, for I had thoroughly ruined all chance of happiness in this world.

Elizabeth Bennet hated me.

I held the watch in my hand, gripping it tightly. I closed my eyes. I did not believe in magic, but if I could, I wished that I could go back in time, to propose to Elizabeth once more. And to do it better this time.

3

MY SECOND ATTEMPT

SOME OF MY readers might wish to know what it feels like to go back in time. My eyes were closed, but I sensed that everything was dark around me like heavy black clouds. For an instant, I was bitterly cold, as if I were naked, standing on the icy surface of the pond at Pemberley in mid-January. I felt slightly nauseated, and then in a moment, everything was calm. I was not cold. I opened my eyes and saw that I was no longer halfway between the parsonage and Rosings. I was standing on the Parsonage doorstep, ready to knock at the door, just as I had envisioned in my mind.

Was this real?

Had I truly gone back in time?

My rational mind argued that this could not be, and yet it was.

I knocked at the door, half fearing that Elizabeth was still angry with me and that she would turn me away.

But no, the maidservant opened the door, just as she had done thirty minutes before. "I will announce you, sir," she said with a curtsey, and I followed her into the house.

Elizabeth stood to greet me exactly as she had done before.

I felt such relief, such gratitude for my father and his magical watch, that I could not help but smile.

For a long moment, I said nothing, and Elizabeth looked at me quizzically. "Mr. Darcy?" she prompted. "Would you care to sit down?"

"Yes, thank you," I said. I would sit down, and this time, I would talk to her calmly instead of alarming her with my hasty proposal. I set my hat and gloves on a table beside me. "Mrs. Collins said that you had a headache. I hope that you are feeling better now."

She frowned a little at my words and said, "I am fine, thank you."

For a moment there was an awkward silence

between us, and then I cleared my throat. I said, "I believe you spoke with my cousin earlier today."

Her eyes narrowed. "I did. The Colonel and I walked about the grounds of Rosings this afternoon."

"And he told you that I separated Mr. Bingley from your sister."

She was surprised by my words. "He did, and I am very angry that you chose to interfere. Who are you to determine how Mr. Bingley is to be made happy? He is not your son or your dog that you can command him."

"You are right. It was presumptuous of me. I should not have interfered." I did not put some of the blame on Bingley for being so easily persuaded.

She was astonished. "You admit that you were wrong?"

"Yes."

"Good heavens, I did not think I would ever hear such a thing from you."

"No, I know that you think I am too proud, with no feelings, but I am sorry if I made your sister unhappy."

"She has been very unhappy. Everyone in Meryton thinks Mr. Bingley was capricious and they look at her with pity, thinking that she has been disappointed in love. Everyone expected him to propose to her."

I knew Mrs. Bennet thought that – she had said as much to Lady Lucas at the ball. It was common knowledge, common gossip, which was the very reason I persuaded Bingley to stay in London and not return to Netherfield. I thought I was saving him from a disadvantageous match.

But now, I didn't care what he did as long as Elizabeth was no longer angry with me. I asked, "Does your sister love Mr. Bingley? I only ask because when I observed her at the ball, I thought that she liked Mr. Bingley and received his attentions with pleasure, but that her heart was untouched. She has such a calm, cool air."

"She does care for him deeply, but she is more reserved. She is not as open as I am."

That was one of the things I loved most about Elizabeth – the way she spoke the truth, even when it was painful. I said, "Then I am truly sorry, and I will speak to Bingley when I am back in Town. I will recommend that he return to Netherfield as soon as possible. I have no doubt but that he will court your sister, because he often speaks of her fondly."

Elizabeth looked at me as if dumbfounded. "You would do that?"

"I would. I want to make amends, because I want both Mr. Bingley and your sister to be happy."

"Oh. Then I thank you, sir. Is this why you came to speak to me, to ask me about Jane and her feelings?"

"In part," I said carefully. "The other reason I came was to tell you how ardently I admire and love you."

Her mouth opened in shock and she gave a little laugh. "Whyever would you do that?"

This time I did not mention her family. I reached over and took her hands in mine. "Because I adore you, dearest, loveliest Elizabeth. I admire your mind and your warm heart. I believe we could be very happy together and I beg of you to consider my proposal."

For a long moment, she did not speak, but then she gently tugged her hand out of my grasp. "Mr. Darcy, I thank you for your sentiments and the honor of your offer, but I must decline."

"Why? Is it because of what Mr. Wickham has told you?"

"Somewhat."

I fought back a rising tide of anger. "Mr.

Wickham is a charming and well-mannered man. I do not expect the world to know how wicked and vile he can be, but I have known him since we were young children because his father was my father's steward. His father was an amiable, honorable man, but Wickham is full of vice and deceit. He gambles, he drinks, he takes advantage of young women. He has been a liar for years, and I regret that you had the misfortune to make his acquaintance."

Elizabeth seemed amazed by my vitriol. "What of the living your father promised him? How can you defend yourself on that?"

"If you knew Wickham as well as I do, you would know that he has no business becoming a clergyman. He would be more likely to seduce the young women in his parish rather than save them. When my father died, the living was promised to him, yes. But Mr. Wickham decided he would rather study the law, and so, in exchange for giving up that living, he received three thousand pounds."

Her eyebrows rose. "So much?"

"Yes. And that was in addition to a thousand pounds he received from my father as a legacy outright. So, he had four thousand pounds which should have been sufficient to establish him in any profession he chose. But instead, he wasted the money. I assume he spent it at the gaming tables and in brothels, for that was his habit for years."

She frowned at my choice of words. "I find this hard to believe. Mr. Wickham appears to be a gentleman."

"I know. He has all the appearance of goodness. You had no reason to doubt him or suspect his motives. However, I know him better. This past summer, he tried to elope with my younger sister, Georgiana. She was only fifteen, which must be her excuse. She had gone to Ramsgate with a Mrs. Younge, as her companion. Mrs. Younge was one of the teachers at her school. However, Mrs. Younge knew Mr. Wickham and together they plotted to seduce and ruin Georgiana."

Elizabeth's face grew pale. "Oh no."

"Mr. Wickham followed them to Ramsgate. Georgiana remembered Mr. Wickham fondly from her childhood, and he preyed upon her tender heart. He convinced her that she was in love with him and persuaded her to elope."

Elizabeth knew as well as I that eloping to Scotland was a scandal. "Is it possible that he truly loved her?"

"He wanted revenge upon me and her dowry," I said flatly. "Mr. Wickham's tastes run to Cyprians and harlots, not girls still in the schoolroom. Fortunately, I arrived the day before they planned to leave. Georgiana is a sweet girl and she could not keep a secret from me. She told me of their plans, hoping that I would give my blessing for their union, perhaps even arrange for them to be married at Pemberley so they would not have to elope. But I knew Wickham's true nature, and I shared some of his dissolute history with her. I dismissed Mrs. Younge, sent Georgiana back to London, and dealt with Wickham as well. I never thought I would see him again until that day you saw us meet at Meryton."

"How can I know that this is true? And not just a tale to make me distrust him?"

I could not blame her for doubting me. "I swear it. And you may speak to Colonel Fitzwilliam, who is also Georgiana's guardian, if you want further confirmation of everything I have said."

Elizabeth held up her hand and said, "No, I don't need any other words. I believe that you are telling me the truth." She looked distraught and I was sorry that I had to tell her such a distressing story.

"Now that you understand that I have not

unjustly harmed Wickham, can you see me differently and accept my proposal?"

Elizabeth said, "No, it is too much to consider at once. I can tell that you are not a villain and I am sorry that I judged you so harshly before."

"You had every reason to."

"But that does not change my answer. I appreciate your offer, but I don't think we would suit. You are a wealthy gentleman. You are accustomed to living in society. I am too rude –"

"Nonsense. You are everything gracious."

"No, I am not. I am afraid that when your passion for me wanes, I would embarrass you."

"My love for you will never die."

She shook her head. "That is not true. The passion of youth always cools. I have only to look at my own parents to see that. In time, I fear that you would regret your choice. I know that my mother would embarrass you. I have seen the way you look at my family with disdain. You think my mother is foolish and vulgar. You would not want your friends to meet her."

That was true, but I said boldly, "My love for you is stronger than any differences between us."

At these words, she looked sad. "Again, I appreciate the sentiment, but I do not return your affections. When we first met, I thought you were too proud. I overheard you telling Mr. Bingley that I was not handsome enough to dance with."

The more she spoke, the more I saw that this second proposal could fail as well. "I apologize for that. I was annoyed with Bingley and I hate to dance."

She smiled wryly. "And yet, you danced with me at the ball at Netherfield."

"I did, and it was one of the happiest moments of my life to have you in my arms, if only briefly."

At this, Elizabeth stiffened, and I knew I had said too much. "Again, sir, I think it best if we end this conversation. I do not love you, and I will not marry for any other reason."

I could hear the finality in her tone. "Do you hate me?"

She hesitated a moment. "I thought I did, but now I am not so certain. I wish you well, Mr. Darcy, and hope that you can find someone else to make you happy. But I am not that woman."

There was nothing more to be said. She did not love me. She did not like me. My wealth and position meant nothing to her.

I supposed that I should be grateful that she did

not say I was the last man on earth that she could ever marry, but her words were still painful.

I stood. "Thank you, madam. Forgive me for having taken up so much of your time and accept my best wishes for your health and happiness."

I bowed and left the room, eager to put her behind me.

I walked back to Rosings in a daze, my thoughts in a turmoil.

When I returned, I went upstairs to my bedroom, rather than join my aunt and cousins in the drawing room. I pulled out a piece of paper, wanting to write a letter to Elizabeth, to explain myself, but there were no words. There was nothing more I could say.

The next day, Lady Catherine cornered me after breakfast. "I know you plan to leave this morning, but shouldn't you speak with Anne first?"

I shook my head. "I have nothing more to say to Anne."

Lady Catherine persisted. "She is waiting for a proposal."

I let my breath out slowly. For years my aunt had said that she wanted me to marry my cousin, who was only a year younger than myself. She said that it was the dearest wish of my mother and that they had planned the union when we were in our cradles.

But I never wanted to marry Anne and she did not want to marry me or anyone else for that matter. Anne was thin and sickly, and she thought that marriage would be too much of a bother. "No," she had told me once. "I want nothing more than to sit in the garden and read my books. When I inherit Rosings, I will become a hermit."

Not that I could tell her mother that. Lady Catherine hired new doctors every year to see what they could do to help Anne.

I said to my aunt, "I need to leave. I will see you again next year for Easter."

I could see that Lady Catherine was disappointed, but she did not press me further, perhaps sensing that if she did, that I might refuse to marry Anne out right.

As I rode away with Richard in the carriage, he said, "What is wrong? I know you are usually quiet, but you haven't spoken more than three words together all day."

I had been thinking about my two proposals all night, wondering how I could have made them better, but I could see that I had not taken sufficient time to win Elizabeth over. I needed time to woo her, to make her see me in a different light.

I needed to show her that I was not proud, and that I did not despise her family – even if I did. I needed to woo her.

But how?

And more importantly – when?

An hour later, I took the watch in my hand and held it tightly in my fist. I closed my eyes and imagined myself back at Rosings that first morning, when Lady Catherine told me that Elizabeth was visiting Mrs. Collins.

4

———————————

MY THIRD ATTEMPT

I OPENED my eyes and I was seated at the breakfast table at Rosings. Lady Catherine said, "My clergyman, Mr. Collins has recently married. His wife was from Hertfordshire. Her father is Sir William Lucas. He is currently visiting, along with Mrs. Collins' younger sister Miss Maria, and a friend of hers, a Miss Elizabeth Bennet."

I smiled. I could do better this time. Now that I had already seen Elizabeth, had already proposed to her twice, I could be more at ease. I said calmly, "I know Mrs. Collins. I met her last autumn when I was visiting Bingley. I met Mr. Collins, too, although our conversation was brief. I should make a call on them this morning. It is the polite thing to do. Richard, would you like to go with me?"

He looked astonished but agreed to accompany me.

This time, I made a better showing at the parsonage. I complimented Mrs. Collins on her home, and I asked Elizabeth about her family. When she asked me if I had ever seen her sister in London, I said that I had not. I did not tell her that Miss Bingley had told me that Jane was in Town and that together we had kept that information hidden from Bingley. Instead I asked Elizabeth if she ever went to Town, and we talked about her uncle, Mr. Gardiner.

As we left the house, Richard said, "What has come over you, Darcy? I have never seen you so loquacious. If I did not know better, I would suspect that Lady Catherine put wine in your cup this morning instead of tea."

"Do not worry, I am not foxed," I assured him. I was inebriated, but not with wine. I was inebriated by Elizabeth Bennet.

The next few days followed a similar pattern. I made a greater effort to speak with Elizabeth. We talked about books and music. I asked her more about her family and told her about mine.

One night, she came to dine at Rosings and after dinner, she played the pianoforte. I offered to turn the pages for her and for a few moments we were alone. No one could overhear us. Before she began the piece, she looked at me quizzically.

I asked, "What is it?"

"I do not know what to make of you, Mr. Darcy. You seem happier at Rosings, more at ease than you were at Netherfield Park. It is a marked difference, almost as if you are two different men. I wonder whatever could be the cause of it."

I smiled. "I hope I am less arrogant now."

She laughed a little. "I did not say that you were arrogant."

"No, but you thought it. Do not lie. I know I made an ass of myself at Meryton. All your neighbors thought I was too toplofty. I am certain they thought I was the proudest, the most disagreeable man in the world."

She looked down. "It is true that you did not show to full advantage."

"No, I did not. And it was my fault. I don't always do well in crowds. I do not have the talent, which some people possess, of conversing easily with those I have never seen before. I cannot catch their tone of conversation or appear interested in their concerns as I often see done."

Her beautiful eyes looked directly into my own. "Are you shy?" she said in astonishment.

"I hope not, but I was not at my best when I first met you, Miss Bennet. I hope I am doing better now."

She blushed.

"What is it?" Lady Catherine demanded. "Miss Bennet, why are you not playing? Is something wrong with the pianoforte? Or are the musical selections too difficult for you?"

"No, they are fine, ma'am," Elizabeth said loudly and began to play, ending our *tete a tete*.

I MET Elizabeth the next morning during one of her walks and asked if I could join her. She nodded. "Do you like to walk?"

"Yes, I like it very much." *Particularly when I walk with you.*

We were silent for a while as we strolled, and then I cleared my throat. "Miss Bennet," I said formally. "There is something I wish to say to you that I should have said before, but I was too proud to air my dealings in public."

She looked alarmed. "You do not need to tell me your secrets, sir."

I would like to tell you all my secrets. I said, "At the ball at Netherfield, we talked about Mr. Wickham. My emotions were still raw at that moment, and I did not explain myself as I should have done."

"You do not owe me any explanations."

I stopped for a moment and she stopped as well. "No, I think I do owe you an explanation. You do not know the entire story of my history with Mr. Wickham. You only know his version, and I assume that he has made me out to be the villain."

She looked uncomfortable, but she faced me bravely. "He has said some strong things against you, sir."

"I am not surprised." I then told her all about Mr. Wickham – how we grew up together, his profligate and immoral behavior at college, and my father's bequests in his will.

"Good heavens," she gasped. "How can this be true?"

I told her that I would understand if she did not believe me. "Wickham has charm and all the appearance of goodness, whereas I do not. I think it might be the set of my eyebrows. My sister tells me that I often look as if I am glaring at her, when all I am doing is thinking."

Elizabeth tilted her head to one side as she considered my face. After a moment, she declared, "You do have a serious countenance, Mr. Darcy, but your eyebrows are perfectly fine."

I smiled down at her. "I am glad they have your approval."

We walked another half hour in silence, and then I told her about Georgiana and how Wickham tried to elope with her.

Elizabeth was astonished and suitably horrified. "Did he harm your sister?"

"No, she thinks her heart was broken, but I think she will be fine. In two years, she will have a Season and forget all about Mr. Wickham." I told Elizabeth that if she needed confirmation for what I had said, she could talk with my cousin Richard, who was also Georgiana's guardian. "He knows all of the particulars."

"No," she said quietly. "I believe you. I don't need confirmation."

I said no more, and we ended our walk in silence. This time, I would give Elizabeth a few days to think about what I had said before I stunned her with a proposal.

Two days later, Richard and I went riding and we stopped by a creek to dismount and stretch our legs. Richard said, "Are you going to marry Miss Bennet?"

"Are my intentions so obvious?"

"To me, yes. To Lady Catherine, I don't know. But I have noticed the way you look at the lovely Miss Bennet. Like a cat after a bowl of cream."

"It's true. I would like to lap her up."

"You rogue." Richard punched my arm and laughed at my bedroom wit. "But don't let Lady Catherine see it."

I rubbed my arm. "I won't. I know she wants me to marry Anne, but that will never happen."

"When do you plan to propose to Miss Bennet?"

"As soon as I can. Tomorrow morning, if it doesn't rain, and I happen to meet her on her walk. If it does rain, we must delay our departure until the weather is better."

"Is that why you have extended our stay so far?"

"Yes. I needed time to court her properly."

"Why? Don't you think your income is enough to win her?"

I shook my head. "No. Elizabeth must be convinced that I am worthy of her."

Richard said, "Ten thousand pounds a year makes you worthy."

"You are a cynic."

"And you don't sufficiently value your position, Darcy. Believe me, every young lady in London would be thrilled to marry you."

"Except for those who want a title."

"All right. I concede that," Richard said finally. "Some women want to be a countess. I know that is why my mother married my father."

I did not comment, because I knew it was true. Lady Matlock and the Earl's marriage was not amicable. They lived in separate residences to keep from killing each other.

The next day it rained but cleared in the afternoon. "Time for my tour of the park," Richard announced. I knew he liked to walk it every year.

"I will join you," I told him. There was a chance that he would meet with Elizabeth, and I did not want him to tell her about Bingley and how I had saved him from a bad marriage.

As I had hoped, we did meet Elizabeth. I stared at Richard meaningfully and asked, "Isn't there something you need to do back at Rosings?"

He frowned, then understood what I was trying to say. "Oh. Yes. I beg your pardon, Miss Bennet, but I need to go back. I am sure Darcy here will take good care of you." He bowed and then winked at me as he turned to go.

Brat.

Elizabeth saw some of the interaction between us and said, "You seem to have a private understanding."

I nodded. "I will tell you some day, but not today."

I held out my arm and she look it willingly, a first for us. I loved the touch of her hand on my coat sleeve, even though she wore gloves.

We walked for a while until we came to Rosing's Folly. Sir Lewis de Bourgh had built it years ago, patterning it after a ruined Greek Temple. I thought it was an absurd bit of architecture, but it was pretty, and I wanted a romantic setting for my third marriage proposal.

Elizabeth sat on a large piece of marble column, lying on its side. She took a deep breath and surveyed the land around us. "It is very pretty here. I like the wilder terrain better than the formal gardens closer to the house."

"You will like Pemberley," I told her. "I have two

walks around the grounds. One is only two miles, but the longer one is ten."

She smiled at me and there was amusement in her beautiful eyes. "Perhaps one day I will see it. I know Miss Bingley liked your home very much."

Was she teasing me? I got down on one knee before her and held out my hand. "Miss Elizabeth," I said formally. "I can no longer keep silent. I must tell you how ardently I admire and love you."

I did not say anything more. I waited for her response, watching her expressive face closely. I would not ruin my chances by talking too much.

"This is a surprise, sir."

"I hope not an unwelcome one. Will you do me the great honor of accepting my hand?"

Elizabeth hesitated, and for a moment I feared that I had failed yet again. But then she smiled widely and took my hand in hers. "Yes, sir. I will marry you, although I find it difficult to believe."

I wanted to whoop for joy, but I merely squeezed her hand and brought it up to my lips. "What is difficult to believe?"

"When I came to Rosings, I did not like you at all," she confessed. "But since then, my feelings have made a material change. I find that I am in love with you."

Thank God.

Then I bent down to kiss her, and she leaned forward to meet me. Our first kiss.

Her lips were soft and sweet, and I wanted to wrap her up like a precious gift and carry her away to Pemberley.

But first, there were decisions to be made.

We talked and laughed, holding hands, hardly aware of our surroundings. There was too much to be thought, and felt, and said, to give attention to any other objects. There was no one that mattered in the entire world except for the two of us and our happiness.

I would leave for London with Richard as previously planned and obtain a marriage license. Then I would come back to Netherfield, bringing Bingley and my sister.

Elizabeth would finish her visit with Mrs. Collins and then she and Miss Mariah would take the coach to London, where they would stay one night with the Gardiners. Then, along with Jane, they would travel home to Longbourn.

Elizabeth wanted to speak to her father first, before I did. As she said, "If you speak to him first, he might refuse you, since he knows how much I did not like you." She blushed. "I said you were odious."

I was not offended because all that was behind us now. "We will do whatever you think is best, Elizabeth."

She looked up at me with teasing eyes. "If that is your attitude, I shall enjoy being Mrs. Darcy."

That statement deserved another kiss – if not two.

"How I adore you, darling Elizabeth," I said.

"And I you."

Belatedly I realized that we were nearing Rosings. I let her hands go and said, "We shall be circumspect now."

She laughed a little and reached up to kiss my cheek. She said, "I must go back to the Parsonage or they will wonder what has happened to me."

I stood and watched my love as she half ran, half skipped away, carrying her bonnet in one hand.

Was any man ever so blessed and happy as I was? If so, I do not believe it.

5

MY THIRD ATTEMPT - PART 2

I LEFT Rosings the following morning and as we rode to London, I told Richard all about Elizabeth.

He wished me the best, whole-heartedly. As the second son of an earl, Richard had no property and his wages as a soldier were his only income. Richard needed to marry an heiress to maintain his standard of living. He often joked about finding a rich widow – the older the better – but I knew that that he envied me for finding Elizabeth.

I knew that I was doubly blessed with my position and a magic watch that enabled to me woo and win Elizabeth Bennet.

I wished that my father were still alive so I could tell him about Elizabeth and share my joy, but at least I could tell my sister Georgiana. I knew that she would enjoy having Elizabeth as a sister.

While I was in London, I obtained a marriage license and spoke with Bingley. I encouraged him to return to Netherfield.

He said, "Caroline thinks I should give up the place."

It was obvious that Caroline Bingley wanted her brother to marry Georgiana. She did not want him to marry Jane Bennet. I said, "Netherfield is a pretty property and besides that, I am going to marry Elizabeth Bennet. If I don't stay with you, I will have to find lodging elsewhere."

Bingley was shocked. "You and Miss Elizabeth? I cannot believe it. I thought you did not like her family."

"At first, I did not," I admitted. "But now I am determined to change my ways. I want Elizabeth to be happy, so I will learn to like her family."

Bingley said, "And if I go with you, I will be able to see Jane again. Do you think that is wise?"

I regretted all that I had done before to separate my friend from Miss Bennet. I had learned from Elizabeth at my first proposal that Jane cared for him, so I said, "I may have been mistaken about her feelings for you."

Bingley's face brightened with hope. "Do you think she likes me after all?"

"I do," I said and after that, Bingley was eager to return. Caroline and Mrs. Hurst chose to stay in London, which would make our travel much more pleasant.

Bingley rode along with me and Georgiana.

As we reached Meryton, I debated whether we should stop first at Netherfield or go directly to Longbourn.

Bingley thought it would be better if we went first to Netherfield and washed off the dirt from our travel. But I was so impatient to see Elizabeth, I could not wait. "We look fine," I told him. "Besides, it will be just a brief call. Fifteen minutes."

As the carriage neared the house, I saw that there was a black wreath on the front door and my heart stopped.

There had been a death in the family.

Although it was selfish of me, my first thought was that if it were one of her parents, Elizabeth and I might not be able to marry for six months.

But then again, if it were her father and Mr. Collins inherited Longbourn, Mrs. Bennet might readily agree to a quick wedding so that she and her other daughters could live with us at Pemberley.

Bingley said, "Do you still think we should call?"

"Yes," I said firmly. I was certain that the servants had already seen us through the curtains, and I did not want to insult them by driving away. Besides, whatever the situation, I needed to be with Elizabeth to comfort her in this time of sorrow.

I knocked on the door and a servant answered.

Bingley and I were announced at a sitting room and we saw Mrs. Bennet hastily dry her eyes. "Oh, Mr. Bingley, it is so good to see you again." Belatedly she noticed me. "Oh, and you too, Mr. Darcy," she said coolly. I knew she did not like me. "But you find us, the whole household, in such terrible times."

I said, "We are sorry to interrupt your hour of grief."

Bingley said, "We are very sorry for your loss."

Mrs. Bennet nodded. "Yes. Poor Lizzie. What a tragedy. She was a perfect girl. My heart will never be whole again."

I felt as if the room swayed.

Bingley said, "Darcy!"

I blurted out, "Is she dead? How did this happen?"

Mrs. Bennet said, "It was an accident at Rosings. One of the servants was cleaning a pistol and it went off. We buried her yesterday."

This could not be. My whole world, my only hope, had gone dark.

Somehow, I made it back to Netherfield.

Bingley tried to comfort me. "I am so sorry, Darcy. I know you truly loved her."

I did. I loved Elizabeth Bennet and I would love no other.

I knew I could take hold of the watch and go back earlier in time, but I was not ready yet. I wrote to Anne to tell me all that had happened. Because it did not make sense that a servant would have shot Elizabeth by accident.

I sent the letter by express and within a few days, I had Anne's reply. I tore open the letter, eager to read her words.

MY DEAR DARCY,

I am so, so sorry to tell you what happened.

On the morning that you left Rosings, my mother invited Elizabeth to have tea with me privately.

While she was with us, my mother confronted her.

Apparently, the day before, my mother had seen you kiss Elizabeth outside in the gardens.

My mother demanded Elizabeth to explain herself — to declare if she was engaged to you.

Elizabeth said, "That information, madam, is between Mr. Darcy, my father, and myself. If and when Mr. Darcy is engaged, I believe he will inform you."

My mother was furious. She called Elizabeth an upstart, saying that if she married you, it would pollute Pemberley. She said that no one in society, none of your friends and family would accept her.

Elizabeth was not cowed. She bravely said that it was your choice, whatever the consequences. And that if you were not afraid of what others would think, she would not be afraid either.

"I see that you are determined to have him." My mother accused Elizabeth of using her arts and allurements to make you forget what you owed to yourself and to all of your family.

At this, my mother added that Elizabeth could not marry you, because you were engaged to me.

Perhaps I should have denied it, but my mother was so angry, I was afraid to speak.

Elizabeth said that you were a gentleman, and that if you were engaged to me, you would not propose to her.

At this, my mother lost all reason. She drew out a pistol

and said, "I will not allow it. You will not marry my nephew."

Elizabeth said, "Are you threatening me?"

I said, "Mother, put the gun away. This is madness."

And then my mother fired the pistol and staggered back.

The bullet struck Elizabeth's throat and she immediately fell to the floor.

My mother stood for a moment as if stunned by what she had just done. Then she dropped the pistol.

"Help!" I cried out. "Help! We need a doctor!"

When a servant appeared in the doorway, my mother sent him away. "It was an accident," she said firmly and closed the door so the servant could not see Elizabeth.

I knelt by Elizabeth, trying to help her, but it was too late. She bled out, unable to speak. It was a quick death, so she was not in pain for long.

My mother said coldly, "It was an accident, Anne. You know that."

I turned on her. "All I know is that you killed her."

"I had no other choice. If she married Darcy, you would die an old maid."

I said, "Darcy and I will never marry, mother. Especially not now with what you have done."

My mother said forcefully, "You are to say nothing of this, Anne. It was an accident. We will say a footman did it.

And if you say differently, I will say that you were the one who shot her."

"Good God." I could not believe what I was hearing. "Why would I want to shoot her?"

"Because she was going to marry your fiancé."

At that moment, I knew that I must keep my silence.

For years, my mother has said that I am too ill, too weak. Who would believe my word over hers?

I await your response. I keep to my room now, feigning headaches.

I am frightened of what my mother might do.

Yours,

Anne

WHEN I FINISHED THE LETTER, I was appalled, saddened, horrified.

I knew that my aunt wanted me to marry Anne, but I never thought she would go to such lengths to make it happen.

And to think of my own dear, sweet Elizabeth lying in her own blood.

I could not think of it.

I could not endure the pain.

I would make certain that Elizabeth was never near Lady Catherine again.

I took my father's watch into my hand and closed my fingers over it, forming a fist. I closed my eyes and wished that I was back at Netherfield, at the beginning of Bingley's ball. I would make certain that instead of going to London afterwards, Bingley would remain in Hertfordshire.

6

MY FOURTH ATTEMPT

WHEN I OPENED MY EYES, I was standing in the entrance hall at Netherfield Park as Bingley greeted his guests. I watched as the Bennets arrived, and praise be to God, there was Elizabeth alive and well again, so beautiful and elegant in a high-waisted yellow gown. She looked about the room, specifically at the officers, possibly looking for Mr. Wickham.

But that did not bother me. I knew that if I had enough time, I could make Elizabeth see reason and she would fall in fall in love with me again.

I could hardly wait to speak with her.

Impatiently, I watched as she danced the first two dances with Mr. Collins. I had to hide a smile. Mr. Collins was a very poor dancer, often going the wrong way, which mortified Elizabeth. *My poor darling.* I was both sympathetic to and amused by her plight.

After the dances, Elizabeth spoke to her friend, Miss Lucas. I approached them to ask Elizabeth for a dance and she agreed.

I left for a few minutes before the music started, and during this time, I observed Bingley with Jane. Now that I knew what to look for, I could see that yes, Jane did care for Bingley. When he talked with other guests, she kept glancing at him briefly, then looking away to hide the fact that she was constantly aware of him.

When I returned to Elizabeth, I could tell that she was agitated. She did not want to dance with me. I knew that she still disliked me, but I was determined to change her mind. Instead of being awkwardly silent, I made conversation, saying, "It is nice that it is no longer raining."

She smiled briefly.

I asked, "You are amused?"

"I have talked about the weather more than a dozen times tonight. Everyone is talking about the rain."

"It is a safe topic of conversation," I agree. "And

can be tiresome. But you must admit that four days of rain was excessive."

"You disapproved of it?"

"Yes, but when I spoke to God, He ignored me."

She gave a little laugh and looked astonished as if she could not believe that I had made a joke. She said, "He ignored my prayers as well."

The music started, and we began the complicated steps. We took our turn, dancing between the two rows of dancers and then waited for the next couple to make their way down the column. I leaned towards Elizabeth and whispered. "All I can think is that someone in Meryton must have been praying for rain. Who do you think it was?"

"Lady Lucas. She has a large garden and always prays for rain."

"Very well, I will not condemn her. I know you like to walk, so did you brave the elements and go outside with an umbrella?"

"No, it was too damp and cold. I did not want to catch a cold like Jane. So instead, I was confined at home with four sisters and my cousin Mr. Collins. It was dreadfully dull. What did you do?"

"Well, as you can imagine, Mr. Hurst took naps and played cards. Mrs. Hurst played the pianoforte and looked at copies of La Belle Assemblee. Since I am not interested in women's fashions, I chose to hide in the library and occasionally I played billiards with Bingley."

"What did Miss Bingley do?"

"She complained."

Elizabeth's lips trembled as if she was hiding a smile. "My younger sisters complained as well. Four days without visits or visitors. No trips to Meryton. It was raining so hard that we had to send a servant to Meryton for our shoe roses."

I looked down and saw the ribbon roses sewn to her dainty dancing slippers. "Very pretty," I said, and Elizabeth blushed.

Then, as if reminding herself that we could not be friends, Elizabeth lifted her chin defiantly and said, "When you met us in Meryton the other day, we had just been forming a new acquaintance."

"Ah yes," I said calmly. "Mr. George Wickham. I assume he has been telling you what a villain I am."

She blinked, astonished by my casual tone. "Actually, yes, he has."

I smiled down at her. "Well, Miss Bennet, the dance floor is hardly the proper place for me to tell all of the history between Mr. Wickham and myself, but I ask you to reserve judgment until you know more of the facts. You have only heard his version."

"That is true, but his story was very credible."

"I do not doubt it. Mr. Wickham is blessed with such happy manners that he makes friends easily. And you had no reason to be suspicious. But, you have not known him long – only a week?"

She thought for a moment and then said, "Eight days."

I said clearly, "Believe me when I tell you that many people have learned to their detriment, that it takes longer to know Mr. Wickham's true nature."

She frowned. "Are you saying that Mr. Wickham is a liar?"

"I am saying, Miss Bennet, that I want to enjoy this dance with you. Perhaps we can talk about Mr. Wickham another day. If you would like, I would gladly take you for a ride in Bingley's curricle – or we could take a long walk – and I would answer any question you might have."

She was silent for a moment as we continued to dance – coming together and then separating with the motion of the steps. When we came back together, she said seriously. "Mr. Darcy, I have always prided myself on judging a person fairly. So yes, I will give you an opportunity to tell me your version."

This was the Elizabeth I loved. She was loyal to her friends, but she was also intellectually honest. I knew that if I had sufficient time to explain myself, she would believe me as she had before. "Thank you," I said sincerely.

For the rest of the dance we were silent – Elizabeth looking uncertain, and as for me, I cherished the chance to dance with her. In my first life, I did not enjoy dancing, but the more I danced with Elizabeth, the more I enjoyed the exercise.

Later that evening, at the supper table, I overheard Mrs. Bennet talking to her friend Lady Lucas about how wonderful it would be when Bingley married Jane. She said that it would be so convenient to have Jane live only three miles away, and since Bingley was so wealthy, he would be able to throw her other daughters in the path of his wealthy friends.

I watched Elizabeth closely and saw how uncomfortable she was. She whispered to her mother to lower her voice, because she did not want me to hear. But Mrs. Bennet did not care for my opinion. As she said sharply, "What is Mr. Darcy to me, pray, that I should be afraid of him? I am sure we owe him no such particular civility as to be obliged to say nothing he may not like to hear."

As much as I still considered Mrs. Bennet to be vulgar, I was impressed with her attitude. She genuinely disliked me and did not care that I was a wealthy man.

I was also impressed with Elizabeth, when I considered the fact that she would refuse Mr. Collin's proposal the following day. She knew what her mother wanted, what the world would say. Marrying Mr. Collins would be reasonable, but she would have the courage to refuse him because she did not love him.

And frankly, I admired her for refusing my first two proposals also. I wondered how a young woman, with such a mother, had developed her own moral independence? I had never asked Elizabeth if she had read Mrs. Godwin's book, *A Vindication on the Rights of Women*, and yet, she seemed to be living by its principles.

I would take everything that I had learned from my prior attempts to make certain that my fourth proposal was a success.

After the supper, singing was talked of, and Elizabeth's sister Mary volunteered to play. I winced, remembering her poor performance from the time before.

As Mary played as ill as she had the first time, I entertained myself by watching Elizabeth's face. She was mortified and embarrassed. Mary had chosen a piece beyond her skill, and her voice was thin.

After one song, when Mary should have retired, she started up again. I watched Elizabeth look at her father entreatingly. He took the hint, and when Mary had finished her second atrocious song, he said, "That will do extremely well, child. You have delighted us long enough. Let the other young ladies have time to exhibit."

I heard Miss Bingley and Mrs. Hurst giggle at his poor manners, but I had some sympathy for him. Mr. Bennet was a quiet man and seemed ill equipped to be a father to five young women.

Elizabeth had said that the love between her parents had waned. Mr. Bennet and Mrs. Bennet were unevenly matched, but I felt that Elizabeth and I would be more simpatico.

This night, I watched as Mr. Bennet ignored his wife and made jokes about his silly daughters. He did not dance, and after a while he retreated to the gaming tables.

Mrs. Bennet watched him go with a disappointed look that she quickly hid with a bright smile for her friends.

For the first time, I felt a twinge of sympathy for her. Mrs. Bennet was no scholar, but she still cared for her husband and did not deserve his derision.

I saw that I would have convince Elizabeth that I was nothing like her father. I would be kind to her family.

I would show her by my actions that my love would last.

After Miss Mary, Mrs. Hurst played the pianoforte. It occurred to me that Mary might play better if she had better instruction. That was something I could arrange once I married Elizabeth.

While I considered such matters, Mr. Collins approached me to introduce himself and to tell me that my aunt, Lady Catherine, was well when he saw her last.

When we had this conversation the first time, I was offended because for Mr. Collins to introduce himself was a breach of etiquette. I had no patience because he was a silly young man who flattered my aunt. And frankly, his sermons were an ordeal to listen to.

However, this time, as he approached, I realized

that I did not mind him at all. Instead, I was grateful to him. I knew Mr. Collins was going to marry Miss Lucas, and I appreciated the fact that his marriage had been the means of Elizabeth meeting me at Rosings.

If Elizabeth had not come to Kent, what would have become of us?

Would I have spent the remainder of my life thinking about that pretty young woman in Hertfordshire?

Or missing her, would I have persuaded Bingley to return to Netherfield?

I did not know, and the thought of losing Elizabeth frightened me.

After Mr. Collins made his awkward introduction, I smiled at him and said it was good to meet him. I thanked him for the news of my aunt and asked him whether it was difficult to work for Lady Catherine because she held such strong opinions. "I imagine that she takes an eager interest in your sermons and your work with your parishioners."

He explained that yes, indeed, Lady Catherine was very active and interested in everyone in the neighborhood. And over time, he had learned which sermon topics were her favorites.

As I spoke with him, I glanced to find Elizabeth

and saw her looking at me with surprise. I thought, *Yes, my dear, I am not what you thought I was. I can be civil, even with your annoying cousin.*

Eventually, the party ended, and as the other guests left, I had to admire Mrs. Bennet's determination. Bingley mentioned that he was planning to go to London, and she was determined to have him commit to a family dinner when he returned.

I also noted that somehow Mrs. Bennet – or should I call her Mrs. Machiavelli? – arranged for the Bennet carriage to be the last to arrive, giving Jane more time to talk to Bingley.

Mrs. Hearst and Miss Bingley complained of fatigue.

Miss Lydia said loudly, "Lord, how tired I am," accompanied by a violent yawn.

I did not know Miss Lydia well, but she seemed strong willed and perhaps reckless. She was the one who encouraged Bingley to host a ball and she seemed often to have her way.

After watching the family more closely, I noticed that Mrs. Bennet praised Jane for her beauty, but in all other ways, she favored Lydia.

Could that be because Lydia was the most like Mrs. Bennet when she was younger?

It was food for thought.

I did not mind that the Bennets were the last to leave, because I treasured every moment with Elizabeth, even if we did not speak.

I was still so grateful that she was alive and well, even if she did not like me.

7

MY FOURTH ATTEMPT – PART 2

IN THE MORNING, I spoke to Bingley over breakfast, which was more of a luncheon because we went to bed so early in the morning. Bingley was planning to leave for London, and I said, "I don't think you should go."

He was astonished. "Why not?"

"Is the business matter so important? Can it not be handled by a few letters?"

Bingley said, "I suppose so, but I like to get things done in person."

Having seen some of Bingley's letters with his poor handwriting, I could appreciate the wisdom of that, but I said, "I think you should stay here and go to the dinner with the Bennets. Jane Bennet is a pretty girl and if you go off to

London, who knows what will happen while you're gone?"

Bingley looked alarmed. "What, are you saying that someone else might snatch her up?"

"All I am saying is that you were not the only gentlemen watching her with approval at the ball last night."

"Who? Who was it?"

I had him hooked now. "I am not going to name names. All I am saying is that Jane Bennet is a beautiful girl, and I don't think you are the only one who admires her."

Bingley said, "You're right. I need to make my intentions clear. I love her. I should not wait. I should move forward. Is that what you think, Darcy?"

He looked at me for advice as if I was his father. I felt a moment's guilt. Bingley was young. Was twenty-two too young to marry? Was I wrong to encourage him?

But on the other hand, I knew that if he married Jane, it would give me more opportunity to woo Elizabeth.

Besides, Elizabeth already told me that Jane loved Bingley.

And truthfully, they were both such good-natured people, they would probably be very happy together. Bingley would never raise his voice, never argue. Jane would never complain.

I envied Bingley because his courtship would have no obstacles.

But I knew I was more fortunate. Winning Elizabeth would be more difficult, but she was the greater prize.

So, we both remained in Hertfordshire and later that day, Caroline Bingley spoke to me privately. "I thought Charles was going to London."

"He changed his mind."

She said, "This is not good. Did you see how he behaved last night? Every two minutes he was at Jane Bennet's side."

"Why don't you want your brother to marry Miss Bennet?"

She demurred. "Naturally, Charles may marry as he pleases, but I don't think Jane Bennet is good enough for him. She is a sweet girl, but her family is atrocious."

I was appalled that I had once agreed with her.

Caroline added, "Part of me always hoped that Charles would fall in love with your sister Georgiana."

"Georgiana is much too young for that."

Ever since she had nearly run away with Wickham, I was in no hurry for her to get married. She needed to become a rational creature before she committed herself to anyone.

Miss Bingley added, "I know, but I am a romantic at heart. Georgiana is such a sweet girl, and I want her for a sister."

Miss Bingley looked at me meaningfully and I knew that she wanted to marry me – which would be another way to have Georgiana as a sister.

But I did not respond to her hint. I said, "Georgiana and Bingley are more like brother and sister. He would not be happy with her."

Miss Bingley retreated. "Whatever you think is best."

A FEW DAYS LATER, we attended the family dinner at Longbourn. While I was there, there was talk of Mr. Collins being engaged to Miss Lucas. Mrs. Bennet could not hide her unhappiness. She glared at Elizabeth and said that Miss Lucas would have never gotten engaged if Lizzy had done her duty. "I don't understand what he saw in her. She is not a beauty."

I said, "I think Mr. Collins has chosen well. Miss Lucas strikes me as a calm, efficient young woman, and I think she will make an excellent wife to a clergyman."

Mr. Bennet looked at me as if surprised by my comment but did not answer.

As I walked past Elizabeth, I said in a low voice, "And I am very glad that you refused him."

Her eyes widened, but she remained silent and looked down at her hands in her lap.

I made a point of complimenting Mrs. Bennet on the meal and playing backgammon with Mr. Bennet. I let him win, which put him in a better mood.

Over the next week, we met again, dining at Netherfield and then at Lucas Lodge. One fine day, Bingley and I went to Longbourn to invite any of the young women of the household who wished to go for a walk. Miss Mary said it was too cold. Mrs. Bennet arranged for Jane to go with Bingley and asked Elizabeth to go with me, which suited me fine. She made certain that both of her daughters were properly dressed with coats, bonnets, and wraps.

Once we were down the road, I said quietly to

Elizabeth, "Let us slow down and let Bingley have his time alone with Jane."

She looked at me with alarm. "Good heavens. Is he going to propose?"

I smiled. "I think so. I hope so."

"Oh how marvelous," she said and beamed at me. My heart thrilled. I wanted to make Elizabeth happy any way that I could.

We walked in silence, keeping our distance from Bingley and Jane, and I remembered all of our walks at Rosings. I now knew more about Elizabeth than she knew about me, and I needed to remedy that.

Elizabeth turned to me and said, "At the ball, you said that you would tell me more about Mr. Wickham. We have the time and the opportunity now. No one else will overhear us."

I was grateful that she wanted to know more. As we walked, I told her about our childhood, Wickham's history of bad behavior, his choosing not to become a clergyman and that he was paid for the living that he gave up. I told her that my father saw the good in him, but that I, as a closer companion, had been able to see his flaws.

Elizabeth was shocked, but she listened closely and asked many questions. After I was finished, she said, "I understand now. That is very different from what Mr. Wickham told me."

"Well, that is what he does. As I said before, he is very charming, and it is a shame because he takes advantage of young women. Perhaps I should have said something earlier, but I did not want to air my private dealings before the world."

"I won't tell anyone."

I smiled. "I know that. But I also don't want him to harm any of your family." I told her about Wickham nearly eloping with Georgiana.

Elizabeth was suitably shocked, as I knew she would be, and she said solemnly, "It is no wonder you hate him."

I told her that she could tell Jane and her father if she thought it would be helpful.

"I will."

As I predicted, Bingley did propose to Jane, and they decided to marry early in the new year. Mrs. Bennet was all happiness, and there was no more castigating Elizabeth for refusing Mr. Collins.

For Mr. Collins was only a clergyman and Mr. Bingley had four thousand pounds a year.

I wrote to Georgiana, who was currently at Darcy House, to tell her that I would be staying in Hertfordshire for two more weeks, but that I would come before Christmas to fetch her. We would spend Christmas at Netherfield and remain there for Bingley's wedding.

Originally, I had gone to London at the end of November and had spent several weeks, taking Georgiana shopping and to plays, but for this attempt, I needed to spend more time with Elizabeth, although I did not tell Georgiana that.

Georgiana wrote back to say that she missed me and to give Bingley all her good wishes.

I was encouraged because every day, it seemed that Elizabeth liked me more.

I met her aunt and uncle, Mr. and Mrs. Gardiner, who came with their children to spend Christmas at Longbourn. Mrs. Gardiner was an elegant, graceful woman. We talked about Lambton because she spent much of her youth there, and she knew a little of my father. Mr. Gardiner was in Trade, but he was intelligent and cheery, and I enjoyed listening to his opinions.

We talked about fishing, of all things, because he enjoyed fishing, as did I.

I invited him to come to Pemberley in the summer. "I think you will like it very much."

"Thank you, sir."

I glanced over at Elizabeth who was watching us with a smile.

Then one evening, we all met for cards at the Philips' home and some officers were there, including Wickham.

The scoundrel blanched when he saw me, but he bowed his head slightly and said insolently, "Mr. Darcy."

I stepped closer to him and said in a very low voice, "Mr. Wickham, I have nothing to say to you. I assume neither of us wish to cause a scene tonight, but I recommend that you give me a wide berth."

Half an hour later, Wickham made his excuses and left the party, accompanied by his friend Mr. Denny.

Elizabeth glanced at me, concerned, and Lydia said loudly, "What happened? Why would anyone leave a party early?"

Two days later, Elizabeth told me that Wickham had resigned his commission and left Meryton. The local hens gossiped, but I thought *good riddance.*

On another evening, I played chess with Elizabeth's father and we discussed history and philosophy.

Elizabeth sat nearby, sewing, occasionally talking to one of her sisters.

I remembered a time when I had been listening to her conversations, so I teased her, saying, "Don't you think I expressed myself quite well just now?"

And she said, "Actually, I do. When we first met, you seemed more taciturn, but now you converse delightfully."

Mrs. Bennet, overhearing us, agreed. "I think you are becoming accustomed to our country ways, Mr. Darcy."

I said, "Perhaps I am, ma'am. I am not generally talkative when I first meet people, but the more I know them, the more comfortable I am."

Elizabeth often took walks in the morning, and I walked near Longbourn with the hope of meeting her. With every conversation, I felt that we were becoming closer.

On the day before I was to go to London, I called at Longbourn and offered to take Elizabeth for a ride in Bingley's curricle.

Mrs. Bennet thought it looked as if it might rain, and Elizabeth brought an umbrella.

I drove out to Oakham Mount and there, I turned to my love. "Miss Bennet, I must tell you how ardently I love and admire you."

Elizabeth's eyes widened and I had a moment's fear. "Have I spoken too soon?"

"No, sir," she said with a smile, and I thought they were the sweetest words I'd ever heard.

I took her hands in mine and kissed them. I looked into her beautiful dark eyes and said, "Can you love me? Will you marry me?"

She nodded. "Yes," she said and laughed a little. "My mother will be astonished."

"Why?"

"Because I did not like you at first, and now I do."

I quickly apologized for the slight at the Meryton Assembly. In her happiness, Elizabeth freely forgave me.

I said, "I can get a special license. Would you like to marry at the same time as Bingley and your sister?"

She blushed. "That would be very nice."

At this point, I untied the ribbons on her bonnet and kissed her.

It was as wonderful as I remembered. For a long time, I held her close, so glad that she was alive and mine. "I want to spend the rest of my days with you, dearest, loveliest Elizabeth. I will protect you.

Life is short, and I plan to cherish every moment with you."

She boldly returned my kiss and said, "You have surprised me, Mr. Darcy. I always thought that you were more of a logical man and not a romantic."

"Can I not be both?"

"I suppose so," she said primly, and I kissed her again.

I would have spent the rest of the afternoon kissing her, but I did not want to scandalize her neighbors, so after a while, we returned to Longbourn, where I requested a private audience with Mr. Bennet.

He was happy to give me permission. When Mrs. Bennet learned of our engagement, she gasped and clasped her hands to her bosom. For a moment I feared that her palpitations might be the death of her. But then she said happily, "Oh, Mr. Darcy. It is too much. Too much. Two daughters married? I shall be distracted."

I glanced at Elizabeth and saw her amusement.

Mrs. Bennet shook her finger at me. "But I am not surprised. I suspected that you cared for her. I think you fell in love with her at Mr. Bingley's ball, am I right?"

I smiled at her. "I think you are right, Mrs.

Bennet. After all, dancing is the first step towards falling in love."

"Exactly!" Mrs. Bennet said with approval. "That is what I always say." She turned to Elizabeth and gave her a hug. "Oh, Lizzy," she cried, "I will miss you when you are so far away in Derbyshire."

I said, "You shall have to visit us at Pemberley."

"And at your house in London?" Lydia prompted. "Can we go there, too?"

Elizabeth frowned, fearing that I would think her younger sister was impertinent, but I said, "Yes, Miss Lydia, you may all come to London, too, if you are on your best behavior."

Mr. Bennet joked, "Then we will never get an invitation."

"Oh, Mr. Bennet," Mrs. Bennet said. "Do not provoke us. Aren't you happy to have Mr. Darcy as a son-in-law?"

Mr. Bennet shrugged and admitted that yes, he was happy for me and Lizzy, but I knew that he would miss his daughter. From what I'd seen, I knew that Elizabeth was his favorite.

THE FOLLOWING DAY I set off for London, full of

hope and happiness. I planned to obtain a marriage license and to fetch my mother's emerald ring for Elizabeth to wear. I looked forward to telling Georgiana my happy news. When I arrived at Darcy House, my butler Mr. Lewis was astonished.

"We did not expect to see you, sir."

I put my hat on a table and pulled off my riding gloves. "And why is that? You knew I was coming for Miss Georgiana. Is she packed and ready?"

"No, sir. She and Mrs. Annesley left for Hertfordshire five days ago. She said she had a letter from you, requesting that they travel by themselves."

"Did you see that letter?"

"No, sir. Miss Georgiana had already tossed it in the fire."

I swore. Georgiana had lied, but why?

I spoke to all the servants to see if any of them knew where Georgiana might have gone.

One of the maids said that she'd seen some letters in Georgiana's fireplace after she'd left.

"Did you see any of the writing?"

"Yes, sir. One of the pages was signed with a 'W.'"

"Wickham?"

One of the footmen said that Mr. Wickham had

spoken to Georgiana at the bookshop. "And you did nothing?"

The man said, "I did not think it a problem, sir, considering the fact that Mr. Wickham was once a welcome guest at Pemberley and Darcy House."

He was correct.

"Also, Mr. Wickham was accompanied by Mrs. Younge, one of Miss Georgiana's teachers. It seemed right and proper for Miss Georgiana to speak with them."

He was right. I could not blame him for Wickham's deceit or for my sister's foolishness.

I quickly wrote to Richard, and together we planned our search for Georgiana. I wrote a letter to Elizabeth, explaining what had happened and that I might not be back in time for Bingley's wedding. "But I still want to marry you, my dearest, and I will return to your side as soon as I am able."

Richard searched London and I went North.

I feared that Wickham meant to marry Georgiana in Scotland.

With every passing mile, I blamed myself. I should have invited her to Netherfield sooner. I should not have left Georgiana alone.

I knew she was lonely, but I had put my own

selfish desires first. When Wickham left Meryton, he must have gone to London directly.

And now they had six days' advantage. But I had better transportation and a deeper pocket.

It took me ten days, but eventually I found them at a small inn outside Gretna Green. I knocked on their bedroom door and Wickham answered it. He was unshaven and in his shirt-sleeves with his waistcoat unbuttoned, hanging open. Georgiana wore a nightshift and a lace robe. Her hair hung down on her shoulders. There was a meagre fire in the grate and the remains of a simple meal on a table.

"Hello, Darcy," Wickham said with a smirk. "Come in. I was expecting you."

I stepped into the room, furious with them both. Acting impulsively, I punched Wickham in the jaw and would have inflicted more bodily harm, but Georgiana cried out and pulled at my arm. "Please, Fitzwilliam, don't hurt him. He is my husband."

Wickham staggered back, holding his jaw and laughing at me. "It is too late, Darcy. Georgiana is mine now. And she is most likely with child."

I glanced in horror at Georgiana and she blushed. They had already consummated the marriage. I clenched my hands into fists, hating Wickham for what he had done.

Georgiana said earnestly, "I love him. I have always loved him. I know you don't like him, but he is the one I want."

Mrs. George Wickham. She had no idea what a miserable, selfish husband he would be. "He doesn't love you. All he wants is your dowry."

"Please don't be angry."

"I am not angry with you," I said and glared at my enemy. "I know full well who is to blame here." I wanted to challenge Wickham to a duel. I wanted to kill him. But if I did that, Georgiana would never forgive me.

Wickham said, "There is nothing you can do now."

My eyes narrowed. Wickham was wrong. There was something I could do. I reached for my father's watch.

8

MY FIFTH ATTEMPT

AT THAT MOMENT, with Wickham taunting me, I knew that I should have brought Georgiana with me when I first went to Hertfordshire. If Georgiana was with me, she would have no opportunity to elope with Wickham. But as a precaution, I would arrange for a maid to sleep outside her bedroom door so she could not escape.

Again, the world was dark and cold, and when I opened my eyes I was sitting at White's, playing cards with Bingley. This was several months earlier, in October 1811.

Bingley invited me to Hertfordshire to see his new home. "It is called Netherfield Park, and although it is not as grand as Pemberley, I think you will enjoy yourself."

I asked, "May I bring Georgiana as well?"

He frowned. "I thought she was still attending school."

Bingley did not know about her near elopement at Ramsgate a few months before. I said, "I have taken her from school. She has private tutors now."

Bingley said, "I am afraid she will be bored in the country."

I said, "You needn't worry. Your sisters will entertain her. And she will have her companion, Mrs. Annesley."

"If you say so," Bingley said graciously. "Of course, I would be delighted to see her again."

Rather than travel with Miss Bingley and Mrs. Hurst, I took my own carriage and brought Georgiana, Mrs. Annesley and my valet.

We arrived the day before the Assembly.

Miss Bingley was thrilled to see Georgiana. "What fun will we have dressing you!" she exclaimed.

I was looking forward to meeting Elizabeth and her family, but I was completely unprepared for the transformation of my little sister.

Georgiana at the time was just fifteen years old, but she was tall for her age and sometimes awkward. She was shy and had a habit of losing her bonnets and twisting her gloves into ropes. She had never attended a public dance before, although thanks to Mrs. Annesley and a dance tutor, she knew the steps.

But when Georgiana came down the stairs, ready for the Assembly, I could not believe my eyes.

Bingley said in quiet awe, "Good God."

Instead of wearing an insipid white dress as was the popular fashion back then for young women, Georgiana was wearing one of Mrs. Hurst's elegant gowns. The fabric was a rich rose color that complimented Georgiana's warm complexion, making it glow with health. The waist of the gown was high, right under her bosom, and the neckline was square and low, displaying her throat and much of her decolletage. I was astounded. When had Georgiana's figure matured? She was not a child any longer.

In the past, Georgiana's hairstyles had been simple – her light brown hair arranged in a bun with a few ringlets, but now her hair was high on her head with ribbons threaded through it.

She wore diamond ear bobs that glittered in the candlelight.

For a moment, I held my breath in wonder. Instead of fifteen, Georgiana looked as if she might be five or six years older, ready to fall in love and get married.

I was not prepared for that.

Georgiana misread my silence as disapproval and said nervously, "What do you think? Do I look silly?"

I smiled. "Not at all. You look like our mother, my dear. Absolutely beautiful."

Her eyes glistened with tears and she sniffed. She held a gloved hand to her bosom. "Do you think the neckline is too low?"

Yes, I definitely did. I turned to Miss Bingley and said, "Perhaps a bit of lace would help?"

It was the work of a few minutes to procure some lace and have it tucked into the top of her dress.

I felt a little better with less of her bosom bared.

As in my original life, we were some of the last people to arrive at the Assembly. The music had already begun, and there were couples dancing. I scanned the crowd, eager to see Elizabeth, who stood next to her sister Mary and Miss Lucas.

My heart leapt. How beautiful she was, and how I longed to speak with her. In my mind, she was still my beloved, my fiancé, but in this attempt, we were still strangers and I would have to woo her again.

In the next half hour, we were introduced to most of Bingley's new neighbors, and I smiled to see Mrs. Bennet push her five daughters forward. Jane glanced at Bingley shyly and I saw that she did like him – from their first meeting.

Bingley danced first with Georgiana. I could tell that she was enjoying herself, and I was happy for her, but I did not like the besotted look in Bingley's eyes.

"They make a beautiful couple, don't they?"

I turned to see Miss Bingley who had managed to slide up next to me.

"Georgiana is too young," I said sharply. "I am beginning to think that she should have stayed home."

I then excused myself and walked across the room to where most of the Bennets were standing. Jane and Lydia had already found dance partners.

I asked Elizabeth to dance, she said yes, and we took our turn about the dance floor. I was thrilled to have her in my arms again, but for her, I could see that I was merely another gentleman at the Assembly. We talked about the size of the room and the occupants. I mentioned the weather, and she agreed calmly that it had been fine for several days.

Since Elizabeth did not know me, yet, she did not smile or make a joke about everyone talking about the weather.

I said, "But let us talk of something else less insipid."

Her eyes brightened. "What?"

"Your choice."

She looked at me quizzically for a moment and then asked how long I had known Mr. Bingley.

"We have been friends for years." After this, I was silent, wishing that I could think of something clever to say. Finally, I said, "Mr. Bingley is one of the most sincere gentlemen I have ever met. He has a warm, open manner that I find refreshing."

"Good qualities in a friend."

I agreed. "Unfortunately, many people in society are more selfish and unreliable." I thought briefly of Wickham.

Her fine eyes shone with wry amusement as she asked, "And where are you on that continuum, Mr. Darcy?"

This was the Elizabeth I loved. "Somewhere in the middle, I'm afraid. I am not a saint like Bingley, but I hope I am a good man. I can be generous as well as selfish. I tend to be quiet and reserved in public, and many people consider me haughty or conceited."

"I do not believe it. You are conversing perfectly well with me."

I smiled. "Perhaps you bring out the best in me, Miss Bennet."

Her face colored at the compliment, and she changed the course of our conversation. She said lightly, "Everyone rejoiced when Mr. Bingley moved into the neighborhood. Netherfield Park had been vacant for some time, and we could always use more company."

"That is where we differ," I say. "I tend to want less company rather than more."

"Ah, but you don't understand. Mr. Bingley is unmarried, and everyone knows that a single man in possession of a good fortune must be in want of a wife."

I smiled at her wit. "All the match-making mamas are ready to pounce on him – like fat cats on a mouse. Poor Mr. Bingley."

She smiled. "I suppose it might look like that, but it is human nature, after all."

"To procreate or to marry advantageously?"

Her eyes widened and I realized that perhaps I

should not have been so bold as to mention procreation at our first meeting.

"Both, I suppose."

I appreciated her intellectual honestly. I said, "What of me? I am also a single young man of good fortune. Will the Hertfordshire tabbies come after me?"

"Yes, if you stay here long enough. How long do you intend to visit your friend?"

As long as it takes to win your heart. "I do not know, yet."

She teased, "And are you looking for a wife, sir?"

"Not anymore. For I have found her," I said meaningfully.

Elizabeth gasped and pulled her hand from mine. For an instant she stood as if frozen in place, upsetting the motions of the dance. Then she said quickly, "Forgive me," and regained her position. She said, "I think it would be better if we paid attention to the dance rather than talk. I don't want to step on your toes."

She smiled politely, but she would not look me directly in the eye.

I damned myself for a fool. I had said too much, too soon.

She was now skittish, like a frightened filly.

We remained silent for the remainder of the dance, separating and coming together as the steps demanded.

At the end of the dance, I bowed and tried to apologize, but she said quickly, "It is nothing. No one talks sense on a dance floor. I know you were only joking."

I wanted to tell her that I was not joking. I wanted to tell her how ardently I admired and loved her.

But that was madness. Elizabeth knew nothing of me or my magic watch. If I pursued her too swiftly, she would think I was touched in the head.

So, I retreated, hoping to win the battle for her heart another day.

That evening, after the Assembly, Bingley and the rest of our party drank coffee and played cards in one of Netherfield's sitting rooms. Mr. Hurst was asleep on one of the couches, snoring. Georgiana held a hand up to her mouth to hide a yawn and said that it had been a most wonderful evening, but that her feet hurt.

"Perhaps it is time for new dancing slippers," I said.

Bingley said that the company was pleasant. "Everybody was most kind and attentive. There was no formality, no stiffness, and I soon felt as if I was acquainted with all the room."

Miss Bingley glanced at me and said that she was not impressed. "I am sure you felt the same, Mr. Darcy."

"And what is that?"

"That the company was not up to your standards. It was only a collection of people with little beauty and no fashion. I did not find anyone interesting."

It was something I might have said myself a few months ago, but I was a better man now. I said, "I disagree. There were several people I found interesting."

Bingley smiled. "Anyone in particular?"

"I think the Bennet family could be interesting, and they live only three miles away." I wanted Bingley to pay attention to Jane instead of my sister.

Miss Bingley made a face. "Mrs. Bennet? That vulgar woman? Surely you are joking, Mr. Darcy?"

"Her five daughters are considered the beauties of the county."

Bingley said, "I saw you dancing with one of them. Was her name Mary?"

"No, she is Elizabeth, the second eldest. But I think Jane Bennet, the eldest, is quite pretty."

"I did not notice her," Georgiana said.

Miss Bingley said, "She has fair hair and wore a blue dress."

"Ah, yes," Georgiana said. "I did see her. She was very pretty."

I could tell that my recommendation meant nothing to Bingley, so I turned to the cards and remained silent.

An hour later, we disbanded, with Mrs. Hurst tugging on her husband's arm to wake him, and everyone going upstairs to bed.

Bingley said, "Darcy, would you wait a moment? I would like to talk to you."

I waited and then he said, "I cannot get over how much your sister has changed."

"It was a new dress, nothing more."

Bingley shook his head. "No, she was a child the last time I spoke to her. She has grown into a lovely young woman."

Who wanted to elope with Wickham a few short weeks ago. I said, "What exactly are you saying?"

Bingley took a deep breath. "I know Georgiana

is too young to fall in love, too young to marry as of yet. But I like her very much, and I would like your permission to court her. I will wait as long as you think is necessary."

Bingley was sincere, and he meant well, but his words horrified me. I now doubted his original love for Jane Bennet. Did he ever truly love her, or was it merely convenience? It was as if leasing an estate made Bingley think he was ready to get married.

And he had chosen the prettiest girl he could find – whether that was Jane Bennet or my sister – it did not seem to matter to him.

I said, "Georgiana is too young. If you are still of the same mind when she is seventeen, you may talk to me then. If she loves you, I would give permission, and you could marry when she is eighteen. But no earlier."

Bingley smiled widely. "Thank you, Darcy. I appreciate this. And to think we may become brothers after all."

I loved him like a brother, but at that moment, I was highly irritated by him. Why could he not love Jane as he had done before? I said firmly, "Until Georgiana is older, be a friend to her, not a lover."

"I will do that," he promised, but I did not completely trust him.

I had seen Bingley in love before. When he was infatuated, he acted moonstruck – following a girl with his eyes, sighing and talking about her. If he did that about Georgiana, I would be tempted to take her back to Pemberley.

But if I did that, I would not be able to court Elizabeth.

Inwardly I swore. *Why was my life so convoluted?*

Half of it was due, no doubt, to my father's watch. I remember his telling me that it could be a blessing or a curse.

But this time, I was going to do everything I could to marry Elizabeth before giving up. I had come to realize that each of my attempts to win her were flawed, but that perhaps I had abandoned one of fate's strings too soon.

I refused to give up hope.

If Elizabeth had loved me before, she could love me again.

9

MY FIFTH ATTEMPT – PART 2

OVER THE NEXT FEW WEEKS, I began to feel that my fifth attempt to gain Elizabeth's affections was doomed.

I continued to attend local social events, but Bingley paid almost no attention to Jane. All of his attention was for my sister.

And Miss Bingley made no effort to speak to the Bennets.

When I suggested that she spend more time with Elizabeth's family, she sneered and said that Mrs. Bennet had two brothers in Trade.

This infuriated me because although Miss Bingley chose to forget it, her own relations were in Trade not so long ago. Her grandfather had made his fortune manufacturing barrels, but he had sold his business when her father was a young man.

But that was not my only trouble.

Elizabeth Bennet seemed to have no interest in me. I feared that I had frightened her by practically declaring my love and devotion at the Assembly like some impulsive callow youth.

I knew she had no interest in me, because she avoided me.

Before, in my first life, Elizabeth would watch me from the corner of her eyes and occasionally talk to me in a combative manner. At the time, I thought she was flirting with me, but now I knew it was because I had insulted her, and she disliked me.

But somehow, thanks to the watch, I had managed to turn that dislike into love.

But how could I turn indifference?

I decided that hatred was preferable to indifference, because it was better that she felt something rather than nothing.

One evening Bingley and I planned to dine with the officers. Miss Bingley should have invited Jane to come to dine, but she did not.

I suggested that she invite Miss Bennet so their evening would not be dull with just the ladies. Miss

Bingley scoffed. "How could we ever be dull with your sister here?"

All through the dinner with the officers, I wondered what I could do to save my romance from ruin.

If Jane Bennet did not dine with Miss Bingley, she would not ride on a horse in the rain. She would not catch a cold. And if Jane were not ill, Elizabeth would not come to visit with her brilliant eyes and muddy hem.

When Elizabeth originally stayed at Netherfield, we saw each other three or four times a day. And except for one time when we were both in the library and I stubbornly refused to speak to her, we talked. It was during her visit that I first admitted to myself that I was falling in love with her.

But without her visit, Elizabeth would have no reason to think of me at all.

And why should she? I did not show to advantage in large groups.

As the days passed, I saw other missed opportunities. Mrs. Bennet and her daughters did not visit Netherfield because Jane was not there. Lydia did not tease Bingley about hosting a ball.

When I casually suggested to Bingley that he host a ball at Netherfield, he was surprised. "Why should I? Besides, I thought you did not like to dance."

And Miss Bingley said it would be too much of a bother. "I think it would be better to return to London. I have received several invitations to balls that will be held in December and if you return to Town, Mr. Darcy, you might also be invited."

I knew that there would be dozens of invitations waiting for me at Darcy House, but I did not want to dance.

I wanted to dance with Elizabeth.

Bingley said he had some business in Town, so perhaps it would be best to return before the end of November.

I said nothing, because there was nothing I could say without sounding like a fool.

But it was so infuriating.

How was I supposed to lay the foundation for Elizabeth to know me better?

One day, I took Georgiana to Meryton to buy gloves. She did not need gloves, but I thought a change of scene would be beneficial. Spending too much time in Caroline Bingley's company was not wise.

When Georgiana could not choose between a pair of white gloves or lavender, I said she could have both, which made her declare that I was the best brother.

"Since I am your only brother, it is not much of a compliment."

She giggled as we stepped out onto the main street.

And then Georgiana swayed as if she might faint.

I took her arm to steady her. "What is it?"

She pointed across the way. "Is that George Wickham?"

I looked and saw that it was. Wickham was standing next to Mr. Denny and the two of them were talking to the Bennet sisters and Mr. Collins.

Damnation. I had forgotten that our earlier meeting in the street was today. If I had remembered it, I would have never brought Georgiana into Meryton.

Unfortunately, Wickham looked our way. *Damn his eyes.*

His face grew red in fear, and I am certain mine was pale with anger.

Wickham touched his hat in salutation. *Insolent bastard.*

I turned away, ignoring him, and helped Georgiana into my carriage that was waiting.

Georgiana looked as if she might be ill, and I said, "Don't worry. I won't let him hurt you."

"But what is he doing here? Do you think he knew I was here? Is he following me?"

"I doubt it. He is going to join the militia."

"Did he tell you that?"

"No. We are not in each other's confidence."

She frowned, confused, but I could not tell her that I knew some of Wickham's future, just as I knew my own.

I glanced at my father's watch.

As much as I hated to admit it, this fifth attempt would never be successful.

I had little chance of speaking with Elizabeth again, and I knew that Wickham would fill her head with lies about me.

And Bingley was a besotted idiot. If I continued on my present path, I would have him as a brother-in-law. In and of itself, that was not a terrible future, but I knew that he was supposed to marry Jane Bennet, just as I was supposed to marry Elizabeth.

But how could I make that happen?

Georgiana said faintly, "I don't want to see Mr. Wickham again."

"You won't," I promised and closed my hand over my father's watch.

10

MY SIXTH ATTEMPT

WHEN I OPENED MY EYES, I was in my study at Pemberley, sitting at my desk, and a footman informed me that Mr. Wickham had arrived to see me. I closed the estate account books and set them aside. "Send him in."

Two weeks before, Wickham had written to me, seeking the living at Kympton. The clergyman who had held the appointment before him had recently died. Wickham wrote that his circumstances were exceedingly bad. He had found the law a most unprofitable study, as I had predicted, and he was willing to be ordained, if I would give him the living as my father had intended.

I had found his letter to be a mixture of entreaty and conceit, and I flatly refused his request.

However, Wickham was determined to change my mind, so he came to Pemberley to argue his case in person.

Wickham waltzed into the room with a flourish. "Darcy," he said with false *bon ami.*

"Sir," I said. "Please, sit down."

He sat across from me in a leather backed chair and set his hat and cane aside. His hair was styled back with French pomade and the points of his shirt collar were too high. I supposed that he considered himself a dandy.

"What brings you to Pemberley?" I said coolly, for we had not spoken face-to-face in three years – not since my father's death, which meant that it was once again the summer of 1809.

Wickham smirked. "I know you already wrote to me about the living at Kympton, but because of our friendship, I wanted to speak with you personally."

As if we had ever been friends. The first time Wickham came to Pemberley, I had turned him down outright, but this time, I had a plan to make him leave England. I wanted him far away from Georgiana and Elizabeth, where his lies would never trouble me again.

He said, "You know your father wanted me to have the living."

"Yes, my father thought very well of you. He loved and cared for you and wanted the best for you. But we both know that you would not make a good clergyman."

"I am a reformed man, I swear."

How many times had I heard his swear on his sainted mother's life? I said, "You would be bored if you had to preach and quote scriptures."

"I could do it."

"No," I said firmly. "I don't mean to offend, but I think you are better suited to business than the church."

Wickham leaned forward, intrigued. "I don't understand your meaning, sir."

"I have a property in the America's. I think you would do well to manage it. And in time, if you had the inclination, you could start your own business." I could easily imagine Wickham running a gaming den or a brothel.

Wickham was astonished. "You would do this for me?"

"Naturally," I lied, for at that moment, I had no property in America, but I would gladly purchase some if I could then court Elizabeth in peace.

Wickham said, "I never thought of going to America. Where is it – New York? Philadelphia?"

I waved my hand, dismissing that information as trifling. "I will write to you as soon as the arrangements are settled. But until then, I will gladly pay for your lodgings at Steven's in Bond Street." I reached into a drawer and pulled out a stack of folded pound notes for him.

I could tell from his countenance that Wickham briefly considered asking to stay at the Clarendon instead, because it was a more fashionable – and expensive – hotel, but he held back, not wanting to press his luck. "That is very generous of you, Darcy," he said with uncharacteristic humility as he took the money. "Thank you."

I smiled at him. "It is what my father would have wanted."

THE NEXT TWO years passed slowly. My plan was to go to Netherfield with Bingley in October of 1811 without Georgiana. There, Bingley would fall in love with Jane Bennet, and without Wickham to poison Elizabeth's mind, I should be able to woo her successfully.

But it was unbearable to relive 1809 and 1810, watching Napoleon's armies take over Europe as he had done before. Everyone was scandalized by the Duke of York and concerned for the King and Country when Prinny became Regent.

It was profitable, however, to know that Cribb would beat Molineaux after 34 rounds. There was nothing like a well-placed wager at White's to increase Pemberley's coffers.

I was desperate to see Elizabeth, so I often thought about going to Hertfordshire on my own. What if I rented Netherfield Park – instead of Bingley – a year earlier?

Mrs. Bennet would want me to marry one of her daughters, but what of Elizabeth?

I already knew that she would not care about my fortune, and I had seen how easily she ignored me when I tried to be affable.

No, it would be better if I began as I had at first – with my being insufferably proud, and with her laughing at me.

In the summer of 1811, Georgiana wrote to ask my permission for her to go to Ramsgate with Mrs. Younge, one of her teachers.

I happily agreed to the adventure because there was no Wickham to bother her.

But a week later, while I was at Darcy House, I received an express communication from Mrs. Younge.

Dear Sir:

It is with my deepest regret that I inform you that your sister, Miss Darcy, died on July the 10th.

It was caused by an accident one day when she went swimming. Somehow her swimming gown caught on a board under the surface of the water, and she drowned.

A physician was sent for, and he did everything he could to revive her, but to no avail.

There was more to her letter, but I did not read it that day.

I was undone, distraught.

I immediately travelled to Ramsgate, all the while cursing my pride and foolishness.

Why had I gone back in time?

Who was I to think that I could change fate? That I knew better than God?

Inadvertently, I had upset the proper pattern of events and now Georgiana was dead.

Was God punishing me for my hubris?

I had been taught from my childhood to believe in the Christian God, but sometimes I wondered if the Greeks had it right.

Our lives were nothing but threads that could be twisted or cut at any moment.

Within a day, I was at Ramsgate. I spoke with the doctor who tried to save my sister. I spent hours sitting next to her cold and lifeless body.

Mrs. Young wailed, wringing her hands and apologizing, but I did not blame her.

She was not at fault; I was.

I was the one who had set this history of events in motion.

Selfishly, I had sent Wickham away, not wanting to deal with him, and now my sister was gone.

It never should have happened.

I wanted to throw my father's watch away, but I held onto it because I knew it was my only hope to see Georgiana alive again.

But what I should do better in the past, where I should go, I did not know.

Every one of my attempts had been disastrous; with this one being the worst of all.

I took Georgiana's body home to Pemberley, and she was buried in the family plot, next to my mother's grave.

For three months, I did not leave the estate. I ate little. I rarely bathed or shaved. I drank too much brandy and walked for hours, often taking the ten-mile path.

But in the end, I travelled to London to meet up with Bingley at the club. I wanted to see – I needed to see – Elizabeth.

Bingley knew I was in mourning, but he still invited me to Netherfield Park, and I accepted.

During our ride to Hertfordshire, Miss Bingley cried, saying that she didn't think she could ever be happy again without Georgiana. She missed her so.

I clenched my jaw and looked out the carriage window, not wanting to talk about Georgiana.

The night of the Assembly, I went, but I did not dance. Instead, I watched Elizabeth and her family from a distance. I overheard the gossip, that I was a proud, disagreeable man because I made no attempt to converse with Bingley's new neighbors.

At one point, Bingley left Jane Bennet on the dance floor and approached me. "Darcy," he said. "Perhaps you did not want to come tonight, but I think you should dance. Perhaps it will lighten your mood. I know you are having a difficult time, but one must live."

I was weary of his attempts to cheer me.

He continued, "I believe that if your sister were alive, she would want you to be happy. To appreciate the joys of this life. Perhaps you should dance with a pretty young woman."

I shook my head, but Bingley persisted. "There is one of Miss Bennet's sisters sitting down just behind you. She is very pretty, and I dare say, very agreeable. Do let me ask my partner to introduce you."

"No, thank you. You had better return to your partner and enjoy her smiles, for you are wasting your time with me. I am not dancing tonight."

Bingley followed my advice and I sat for a moment, tormented by my dark thoughts.

But then I realized that Elizabeth, sitting so close, had most likely overheard our conversation. I stood and walked over to where she was seated. I asked, "Do you mind if I join you?"

She smiled at me briefly. "None of these seats are claimed, sir. You may sit wherever you like."

How I had missed her beautiful face — those eyes — and her pretty smile.

I said stiffly, "We have not been formally introduced, but I must apologize. I did not mean to be offensive just now. My refusal to dance had nothing to do with you or your charms."

She lifted her chin. "I didn't think it did."

I said, "If I were more sociable, I would enjoy dancing with you very much, but tonight I am poor company."

"And why is that, sir?"

Looking at the woman I had loved for years, I said bluntly, "My younger sister recently died, and I find that I have little hope for living."

Elizabeth drew her breath in sharply. "I am so sorry to hear that, sir."

I nodded, touched by her sympathy. In a flat voice, I told her that it was an accident and that she drowned.

"Oh, dear. How old was she?"

"She was fifteen. She would have been sixteen in January."

"That is the age of my sister Lydia."

I glanced at the dance floor to see Lydia dancing with a redcoat, one of the officers. She was so full of life and vitality, that it made my heart ache. Poor Georgiana could not dance now.

Elizabeth said, "It is a terrible loss."

"Yes, for she was the last of my family. Both of my parents are dead as well."

"Then you are alone in the world."

She understood me. "Yes."

She said, "It is no wonder that you do not wish to dance. That must be very difficult. But I believe you should take all the time you need to grieve. Do not let anyone tell you to smile and ignore your sorrows. I don't think that is reasonable advice. Every heart heals at its own pace."

I had missed her philosophical insights. I said, "You are very wise for your young age. Have you dealt with sorrow?"

"Everyone has. My sorrow was the death of my grandparents, but I know it was less than yours. They were older. I missed them, but I knew it was time for them to leave. Fortunately, I still have my parents and my four sisters, all living."

She spoke so tenderly, I had to hold back tears. If we were still engaged, I could have held her close and poured out my agony. I knew she would have comforted me.

But we were seated at an Assembly. She did not know me from Adam. I said calmly, "Thank you for listening to me, a stranger. You are very kind."

She smiled briefly. "I should hope that I would listen to anyone in need, whether they were a stranger or not."

I chose to ignore the rules of society and introduced myself. "My name is Darcy. Fitzwilliam Darcy."

"And I am Miss Elizabeth Bennet, but I already knew your name and that you have a large estate in Derbyshire."

I smiled. "Ah, yes, the tabbies know everything about a man within ten minutes of his entering the room."

Elizabeth frowned, making a little 'v' between her beautiful eyes. "Tabbies?"

She did not remember our prior conversations – how could she? I explained. "All the gossiping mothers who are eager to have me wed one of their daughters."

"Oh, I see. Are you often hounded by them?"

"Like a fox at a hunt."

She smiled wider. "I thought they were cats not hounds."

How I loved her – her wit and generous spirit. "That is not all. Some of them are snakes."

Her eyes sparkled and she pursed her pretty lips that I longed to kiss. "True. I have met a few snakes in my life, but I assume there are more in London than in the country."

"Yes, not that the percentage of snakes is actually higher there, but that the population is greater."

"That is reasonable."

For a moment, I basked in the warmth of Elizabeth's regard, but then I remembered Georgiana. How could I talk silly nonsense when my sister lay dead in her grave?

Elizabeth must have noticed the turn of my thoughts, for she said quietly. "You do not need to talk, sir, if you do not wish."

"Thank you."

We sat together for several minutes in silence as the other attendees danced and conversed.

After a while, Elizabeth excused herself and walked over to speak with her friend Miss Lucas. As much as I wanted Elizabeth to stay by me, I knew that was unreasonable. She did not know me. She did not love me.

I glanced at my father's watch, at the hands that did not move.

I believed with all my heart that if I had enough time with her, Elizabeth could fall in love with me again. I could marry her and together we would be happy.

But how could I be happy with Georgiana dead?

I would always know that if I had made different choices, she would still be living.

I could not take my happiness at her expense.

Not for the first time, I wanted to talk with my father.

Now that I understood the watch better, I wanted his advice.

Having already spent two years waiting to see Elizabeth, I knew the risk I was taking. If I went back to speak to my father, I would have to wait five years to see her again. And there was always be the chance that some odd twist of fate would keep us apart.

I glanced across the room at Elizabeth one last time. How beautiful she was – how infinitely precious to me.

Then I took the watch in my hand and closed my eyes.

11

MY SEVENTH ATTEMPT

ONCE AGAIN, I was cold and nauseated, and when I opened my eyes, I was at the door to my father's bedroom at Pemberley. I could hear Georgiana crying in the hallway. I wanted to run to her and hug her, relieved that she was once again living, but I would do that later. First, I needed to speak to my father.

As before, my father lay on his bed with his eyes closed. The room was dark, lit only by the fireplace and a few candles.

"Fitzwilliam," my father said weakly.

I leaned closer. "Yes, sir?"

"My watch."

I glanced down at my fob, but the watch was not there, and I felt oddly bereft. The watch had been my companion for more than five years. It was now resting on the table beside my father's bed. I carried it over my father who then handed it back to me. "It … is … yours … now."

I thanked him and sat on a chair beside his bed, waiting for him to say more.

He said clearly, "This watch can enable you to go back in time."

I nodded and he looked at me suspiciously. "You are not surprised."

"No, sir."

"Is this the second or third time we have had this discussion?"

"Second."

His tone was wry. "Then I do not need to convince you of its efficacy."

"No, sir, I fully believe in its magic now. You said before that the watch could be a blessing or a curse."

"And you feel cursed?"

"Yes, sir."

He sighed. "Tell me about it, son."

"I met the most wonderful young woman. Her name is Elizabeth Bennet, and she lives in Hertford-shire." I was glad to be able to tell him about Elizabeth. It was one of my great sorrows that neither of my parents had known her.

"What color is her hair?"

"Brown."

"And her eyes?"

"Brown, but there are flecks of green."

"Is she pretty?"

"Perhaps not in a classic sense, but for years now, I have considered her one of the handsomest women of my acquaintance."

"Excellent."

"But that is not why I love her. I love her intelligence, her wit, and her warm heart."

"And what happened? Why did you feel the need to talk to me?"

"I was an ass. When I proposed to her, I insulted her family."

My father nodded as if amused. "Ah. What was wrong with her family?"

"Some connections to Trade, but that no longer matters. I was wrong to care about it. The only thing that matters is Elizabeth and her character."

"Very good," my father said as if pleased with me. "So, what happened when you proposed a second time?"

"I was not successful until the third proposal."

"And what went wrong?"

"Lady Catherine shot her."

"Good God," he said. "I assume she still wanted you to marry Anne."

"Yes, sir."

"Don't do it. Lady Catherine would make a terrible mother-in-law."

"Indeed. But do not worry, sir, I will not marry Anne under any circumstance."

"I am relieved," he said dryly. "But please continue."

"I tried several other times, but each time, it was as if my quest was a sinking boat. If I patched one hole, I inadvertently created another." I did not want to tell him that Georgiana had died.

My father said, "That is the curse, yes. We think we know what we are doing, but it is impossible to control every aspect. But tell me more about your Elizabeth."

For the next half hour, I spoke to my father, telling him about my various attempts to win Elizabeth.

He was alarmed to hear about Wickham's villainy. He said, "I never knew his true nature. Forgive me."

"It is all right," I told him. "You saw the best in him. There is no sin in that."

"I wish things could be different, but the watch is yours now. How will you go forward?"

I took a deep breath. "I am thinking that I should live this attempt as I lived the first, making Elizabeth dislike me and letting her refuse me so angrily." I watched my father's face, seeking his approval.

"And then?"

"I will write her a letter and pray to God that we meet again."

My father nodded. "Yes. That sounds wise but remember you can always give God a little nudge."

We both laughed, and my father's laugh became a series of hacking coughs that made his body shake. He winced in pain, and I feared that he would expire then, instead of lingering for another hour.

But finally, he rallied and said weakly, "Do not fear. I have faith in you, Fitzwilliam. Like me, you have determination, and you will not give up."

I treasured his words. "Thank you, sir."

"Now, what else would you ask of me before I leave this frail existence?"

I asked him how he had wooed my mother, and

my father said it had taken nine attempts to win her. He coughed again. "There was a persuasive Viscount who wanted her, but eventually I was victorious." He sighed. "Lady Anne made me the happiest of men. I hope I made her happy as well."

"You did, sir."

I held his hand until he slipped peaceably away.

THE NEXT FIVE years were as hellish as I had anticipated. I tried to act the same as I had done initially, but I had less patience for society's foibles. I spoke less and read more. I did everything I could to improve Pemberley and Darcy House.

Although I encouraged my friendship with Bingley, I was barely civil to Miss Bingley.

I saved Georgiana at Ramsgate and dismissed Wickham and Mrs. Younge. By October of 1811, I was very eager to return to Hertfordshire.

I had spent years thinking about Elizabeth Bennet and how best to win her heart.

I reasoned that I should let her dislike me, let her refuse me, and that I would make amends afterwards.

I knew from my two successful proposals that

once I apologized sincerely, she would listen. And if we had the opportunity to talk and walk together, she could fall in love with me.

At the Assembly in Meryton, it was all I could do to maintain my façade of indifference. When Bingley suggested that I dance with Elizabeth, I said haughtily, "She is tolerable; but not handsome enough to tempt me; and I am in no humor at present to give consequence to young ladies who are slighted by other men."

Bingley just shook his head at me and returned to Jane Bennet.

A few minutes later, I glanced slyly over at Elizabeth and saw her talking with Charlotte Lucas, laughing at me and what I had said.

I was pleased.

12

MY SEVENTH ATTEMPT – PART 2

SIX MONTHS LATER

I STOOD on the front steps of the Parsonage with Elizabeth's angry words ringing in my ears. *You could not have made me the offer of your hand in any possible way that would have tempted me to accept it.*

Before those words were like knives, but today, I was hopeful, and I whistled as I walked back to Rosings.

I thought, *You don't think there is any way I could tempt you to marry me? Well, we shall see, my darling Miss Elizabeth Bennet, we shall see.*

When I returned to Rosings, Richard wondered where I had been, but I prevaricated. "I went for a walk," I said, and then I excused myself to go up to my bedroom.

Once there, I removed writing paper from my desk and opened a bottle of ink. I wrote:

BE NOT ALARMED, Madam, on receiving this letter, by the apprehension of its containing any repetition of those senti-ments, or a renewal of those offers, which were last night so disgusting to you.

I SMILED as I explained myself – firstly, my reasons for separating Bingley from Jane, and secondly, my dealings with Wickham.

I trusted that as long as Elizabeth actually read the letter – instead of tossing it in the fireplace – that its contents would begin to soften her heart.

She would be unable to trust or to believe Wickham once she knew the facts of our history, and as for Jane and Bingley, I would do what I could to bring the two of them together again.

The following morning, I waited outside in one of the groves for more than an hour, hoping to meet Elizabeth on one of her walks.

When I saw her, my heart raced, but she looked alarmed.

I held out the letter and said, "Will you do me the honor of reading this letter?"

She nodded and took it. I bowed, and then turned and walked quickly away, praying that she would read it and thoughtfully consider my words.

Richard and I left Rosings that morning and I returned to Darcy House. I learned that Bingley was traveling in the Lake District, so I had to wait nearly a month to speak to him face-to-face. When I suggested that he return to Netherfield Park, he was reluctant. His sister Caroline had spent weeks trying to get him to give up the property entirely.

Bingley did, however, agree to visit Pemberley in August with his sisters, and I planned to convince him then to go back to Hertfordshire. I would accompany him, and as Bingley courted Jane, I would court Elizabeth.

However, if he refused to return, I would go back alone, by myself, although I did not have a proper excuse, yet.

On my return to Pemberley, I rode ahead from the rest of the party because I had business with my steward. I was walking up from the gardens to the back of the house and to my astonishment, I saw Elizabeth accompanied by her Aunt and Uncle Gardiner. Mr. Gardiner was talking to one of my gardeners.

I started, immoveable from shock, silent from a sudden lack of wits.

Elizabeth was here, before me.

The answer to all my prayers.

I cleared my throat. "Good day, Miss Bennet. How good it is to see you."

She had instinctively turned away but then greeted me politely. I could tell that she was uncomfortable, possibly remembering the vehemence of our last conversation.

I said, "How long have you been in Derbyshire?"

"A few days, sir. We are staying at Lambton."

"Excellent. How is your family? Are they all well?"

"Yes, when we left them."

"How long have you been traveling?"

"Two weeks, sir." She blushed and said, "We came to tour the house, but the housekeeper assured us that you – that the family was not present. I would never have presumed –"

"No," I assured her. "It is no trouble. I was

supposed to arrive tomorrow. I came early to speak with my steward."

She glanced nervously at her relations.

I said, "I am glad you saw the house. I hope you liked it."

"I did," she said, then blushed again.

I felt like a fool. That was a stupid question. What was she supposed to say – that she didn't like Pemberley?

For a moment we stood there, neither of us speaking, and then I awkwardly took my leave.

As I walked to the house, I silently berated myself. I should have said more, done more. Elizabeth Bennet had appeared in my garden like manna from heaven, and I was acting like a lovesick fool.

Once inside the house, I washed my face, quickly changed my shirt and waistcoat, and ordered Mrs. Reynolds to prepare tea for my guests.

I hurried back outside and found them along one of the walks. Elizabeth introduced me to her aunt and uncle. We talked about Lambton and fishing. The Gardiners were as intelligent and gracious as I remembered. I invited them to stay for tea, but Elizabeth declined. "Another day, perhaps," I said, and she smiled.

I had hope now. I don't think she hated me any longer.

THE NEXT FEW days were idyllic. I called at the inn at Lambton and introduced Elizabeth to my sister. Georgiana then invited the women for a tea the following afternoon, and I suggested that Mr. Gardiner come in the morning for fishing.

In addition to the tea party, we also had a dinner together. I watched with joy as Elizabeth and Georgiana became friends. Caroline Bingley was her usual unpleasant self, but I paid her little attention.

Elizabeth often smiled at me, and she seemed to enjoy our conversations. I could tell that she liked my sister, and she liked my house.

But did she like me?

The next morning, I called on her at the inn, wanting to invite her party to a picnic, but when I entered the room, it seemed as if Elizabeth was trying to leave. Her face was red and tear-stained. She hastily exclaimed, "I beg your pardon, but I must leave you. I must find Mr. Gardiner this moment, on business that cannot be delayed; I have not an instant to lose."

"Good God! What is the matter?" I cried, then tried to recollect myself. "I will not detain you a minute, but let me, or let the servant go after Mr. and Mrs. Gardiner. You are not well enough. You cannot go yourself."

Elizabeth hesitated and looked as if she might faint. She called back the servant and sent him to fetch Mr. Gardiner directly.

Once the servant left, she sank down on a chair, unable to support herself.

I said, "Let me call your maid. Is there nothing you could take to give you present relief? A glass of wine? Shall I get you one? You are very ill."

She said, "No, I thank you. There is nothing the matter with me. I am quiet well. I am only distressed by some dreadful news which I have just received from Longbourn."

She burst into tears and I saw an open letter on the table.

Had someone died? Was it her mother or her father?

Either way, I would help her all that I could.

She dried her eyes and said with a trembling voice,

"I have just had a letter from Jane with such dreadful news. It cannot be concealed from anyone. My youngest sister has left all her friends – has eloped – has thrown herself into the power of Mr. Wickham."

Wickham again. I hated that man and all that he had done.

She continued, "They are gone off together from Brighton. You know him too well to doubt the rest. She has no money, no connections, nothing that can tempt him. She is lost forever."

Elizabeth was right. Wickham would never marry Lydia. He would ruin her.

Elizabeth twisted her hands before her. "I could have prevented this. I knew what he was, but I said nothing. If only I had warned my own family, this could not have happened. But is too late."

"You are not responsible for Wickham's actions."

"No, but I should have said something."

I said, "I am grieved, indeed. Grieved and shocked. But is it certain, absolutely certain?"

"Yes. They left Brighton together on Sunday and were traced almost to London. They are not going to Scotland."

No, Wickham reserved Scotland for wealthy young women like my sister.

I said, "And what has been done to rescue her?"

"My father is gone to London, and Jane has written to beg my uncle's immediate assistance."

I thought that Mr. Gardiner would be more helpful than Mr. Bennet.

I wanted to help Elizabeth, but I would not make promises. I did not want to give her false hopes. I could tell that she was distraught, and I feared that my presence was making matters worse. I said I wished her and her family well and then took my leave.

I stopped briefly at Pemberley to inform my sister that Elizabeth would not be visiting that day, and then I traveled to London to hunt down Wickham.

IT TOOK NEARLY two weeks and a large bribe to Mrs. Younge to find Wickham and Lydia. They were living in a small room, poorly furnished, without a fire in the grate. I spoke to Lydia and tried to persuade her to quit her disgraceful situation and return to her family, but she would have none of it.

Lydia was determined to stay where she was.

She refused to leave Wickham because she loved him. She was sure that they would be married at some time, and she did not care a jot when that might happen.

I thought Georgiana had been foolish to marry Wickham, but Lydia was worse because she blithely let him take liberties without a ring on her finger.

She was young and head-strong, taking no thought as to her predicament or possible repercussions.

Part of me was tempted to let her lie in the bed she had made, but I could not do that to Elizabeth. I must try to save her family's reputation if I could.

When I spoke privately to Wickham, he confessed that he had no intention of marrying Lydia. She had been a convenient armful, nothing more. He had left Brighton because of his excessive debts.

He still had plans of marrying an heiress, and if I did not intervene, I knew that he would abandon Lydia without an ounce of compassion.

Lydia's dowry was too small to make him marry her, so in the end, I offered to pay his debts, pay for a commission in the North, and provide him a sum of money to start him in the world if he would marry her.

But before finalizing the terms of our agreement, I met with Mr. Gardiner in Gracechurch Street, and he wrote to Mr. Bennet to get his permission.

By the end of August, it was done.

I was at the church to see Wickham marry Lydia. I was disgusted by their cavalier attitude, but I consoled myself with the thought that at least Georgiana was safe for now.

After the wedding, I returned to Pemberley to fetch Georgiana, and then we went London so I could speak to Bingley. I informed Bingley that I might have been mistaken about Jane's feelings for him, and I suggested that he return to Netherfield as soon as possible.

We arrived in Hertfordshire in mid-September, and Bingley promptly accepted an invitation from Mrs. Bennet for a family dinner.

I could hardly wait to see Elizabeth again.

13

MY SEVENTH ATTEMPT – PART 3

ALTHOUGH I HAD WON Elizabeth's heart twice before, I hesitated to make my feelings known. I did not want to be refused again. So rather than converse smoothly when we were together, I was silent and awkward like a block.

I said nothing when Mrs. Bennet spoke about Lydia marrying Wickham. I had told Mr. Gardiner to keep my part of the affair secret. I did not want Elizabeth to fall in love with me or marry me out of obligation.

After a few days in Hertfordshire, I retreated to London, not knowing what my next steps should be. I knew that Bingley would propose to Jane while I was gone, and I wished him God speed.

However, I was not ready to propose to Elizabeth.

I did not want to use the watch again, so I had to be doubly careful.

While I was in London, Lady Catherine called on me at Darcy House. She had heard rumors that I was in Hertfordshire, courting Elizabeth. I assumed that this gossip came from Lady Lucas and had passed to Mrs. Collins. From there, it was a quick jump to Mr. Collins and Lady Catherine.

Lady Catherine was indignant. As she said, "I knew this must be a false report, but I went to Hertfordshire to make certain of it. I called at Longbourn and spoke to Miss Elizabeth Bennet myself."

I was horrified. "Is she still living?"

Lady Catherine frowned. "Whatever do you mean? Yes, of course she is still living. She is a very disrespectful, insolent girl, and I am sorry I ever met her. I will certainly never invite her to Rosings again."

And I would make certain that Elizabeth never stepped foot on the grounds, either. I asked carefully, "What did you say to her?"

"I told her about the rumors and informed her that you were engaged to my daughter."

I did not want to argue that point. "How did Miss Bennet respond?"

"With impudence. She said that if you were engaged to Anne, you would not propose to her. I then asked her outright if she was engaged to you, and she said that no, she was not. You can imagine how relieved I felt."

Not half as relieved as I was that my aunt had not killed her.

My aunt continued, "I then asked her if she would promise to never enter into such an engagement with you."

"And what did she say?" I knew that if Elizabeth were dead set against me, she would declare it boldly.

Lady Catherine fumed. "She was obstinate. She refused to promise."

This was excellent news.

Lady Catherine said, "I told her that if she was determined to have you, that it would end poorly. That none of your family and friends would accept her. That it would be a scandal. We would never mention her name. I said I knew about her sister's infamous elopement. I told her that you would never let the son of your late father's steward become your own brother."

As if I cared about that. I said calmly, "I am sorry that you went to all that trouble, Aunt."

"It was no trouble if it keeps you from marrying her. I wanted you to know what kind of young woman she truly is."

"Do not worry, ma'am," I said firmly. "I know Miss Elizabeth Bennet quite well, and everything you have told me merely confirms my original opinion of her."

My aunt smiled. "I am glad to hear it, Darcy. I should have known that you would not be swayed by her allurements."

Frankly, I was eager to sample all of Elizabeth's allurements, but I said nothing of that to my aunt. Lady Catherine stayed the night at Darcy House and left for Kent the next morning.

And then I, encouraged by my aunt's report, returned to Hertfordshire.

Upon my arrival, I learned that Bingley was engaged to Jane, and they planned to marry soon. I accompanied Bingley as he called at Longbourn. Together, we took Jane and Elizabeth for a walk. I slowed down, so that Jane and Bingley could have their privacy and Elizabeth and I could have ours.

We said little at first, enjoying the cooler weather, and Elizabeth said, "Mr. Darcy, I must thank you for your kindness to my poor sister. Ever since I have known of it, I have wanted to express my gratitude."

This was what I had wanted to avoid. I wanted her love, not her gratitude. I told her that whatever I had done, I had done it all for her – to make her happy.

She blushed.

Emboldened, I added, "You are too generous to trifle with me. If your feelings are still what they were last April, tell me so at once. My affections and wishes are unchanged, but one word from you will silence me on this subject forever."

Elizabeth hesitated and my heart sank. Had I spoken too much too soon?

It occurred to me that with the watch, I could undo my promise not to bother her again, and she would never know. I could try another time to win her.

She said, "Mr. Darcy, my feelings are not what they were before. They have undergone a material change."

I reached for her hands and held them in mine. "Dare I hope? Do you love me?"

"I do," she said and laughed a little.

"Then you will marry me?"

"Yes." Her brilliant eyes shone with happiness.

"As soon as possible?" I did not want to wait for the banns. I wanted to marry her as quickly as could be. I wanted to secure her, right and tight, where nothing could separate us.

She smiled as if a little bemused by my intensity. "Yes, if you want."

"If I want? If I want?" I repeated incredulously and then I kissed her. Unlike our other first kisses, where I approached her carefully, sweetly, like the gentle unfolding of a flower, this time I pulled her towards me and kissed her ruthlessly with all the passion of a man who had waited years for her.

"Good heavens!" Elizabeth gasped when I finally let her go.

Her bonnet was on the ground and her hair was falling from its pins. Her lips were swollen, a darker pink, and I thought she was the most beautiful woman in the world.

I tenderly touched her cheek. "Have I frightened you, my darling?"

She smiled widely. "Not at all, Mr. Darcy."

14

———————

AT LAST

JANE AND BINGLEY and Elizabeth and I married on the same day. We did not invite Lady Catherine, and as a precaution, I arranged for several armed footmen to be in the congregation just in case she decided to attend.

Mrs. Bennet was so happy to have two more daughters marry, I was concerned that her palpitations might result in apoplexy, but to our surprise, she lived twenty-seven years longer in sufficiently good health and spirits to enjoy her many grandchildren.

Mr. Bennet did not live as long as his wife, but he also enjoyed frequent visits to Pemberley – primarily for our library.

Kitty married one of Bingley's cousins, and

Mary did not marry at all. She became interested in botany, of all things, and developed a new type of rose called the Pemberley.

Lydia and Wickham's union was not particularly happy – her affection for him outlasted his for her, but eventually he caught a violent cold – no doubt while climbing out of some poor woman's bedchamber in the rain – and he died before his thirty-second birthday.

Lydia married again, to a clergyman, and had seven children, all of them better behaved than she had been.

Georgiana had her Season when she was eighteen and married an Irish baronet who raced horses.

As for Elizabeth and myself, there could not be a happier union. She has been everything to me – friend, lover, and mother to my children.

As for my father's watch, I set it aside on the day I married. As much as I have been tempted since then to avoid a specific problem or to relive a particularly happy day or week, I have never risked it.

I decided that I would accept the thread of life that the Fates decreed; I did not dare to alter it, because I had already won the prize.

As Elizabeth and I rode away from our wedding breakfast in my carriage, she handed me a small box.

"What is this?"

She kissed my cheek and laughed. "A wedding present from me to you."

I was surprised. "You didn't need to get me one. You are already my present."

She smiled. "I think you will like it. You will find it useful."

I opened the box and saw a new watch resting on velvet.

Elizabeth said, "I have noticed that you often look at your watch, and it is broken. The hands never move."

I opened the watch case and saw that there was an engraving inside: *Forever yours, Elizabeth.*

I briefly thought of my father and all his wishes for me. I said, "You are right, this is much better."

AUTHOR'S NOTE

I hope you enjoyed this time travel story. I love time travel and I love Mr. Darcy.

And if you would like, please leave a review.

I have many more JAFF stories to tell.

Happy reading,

<3 Ada

www.ingramcontent.com/pod-product-compliance
Lightning Source LLC
Chambersburg PA
CBHW022133150726
47992CB00002B/576